THE QUEEN OF VAN DIEMEN'S LAND

AND OTHER STORIES

ANTHONY WATT

wotco

DEDICATION

These stories are dedicated to those, like Rosa Parks and Mamie, who struggle against the oppression of white supremacy, to those victims of the Scottish Witch Trials, and to those women who suffer oppression in parts of the world today.

Also, my apologies to those innocent victims of my pen:

Social workers

Archeologists

Model Rail enthusiasts

Aspiring actors

Duelling sisters

Dog lovers

I would like to remember former colleagues Edith Sanders and Morris Lindsay.

A number of the stories feature figures from history.

'Three cigars, ninety-five photographs' deals with the Battle of Antietam, fought on September the Seventeenth, 1862. Although the hero, Astrid Karlsson, is fictional, the other main characters are portrayed with accurately. The Union's commanding general, George B. McClellan, was guilty of serious misjudgement by delaying action, which possibly saw the opportunity to end the war lost. The Confederate Special Order 191, a detailed battle plan, was discovered by Sergeant John Boss and Corporal Barton McLean, in the wrapping of three cigars. Mathew Brady's ninety-five photographs - The Dead of Antietam - shocked the nation. On the day following the battle, President Lincoln dismissed McClellan, who never again commanded an army. That same day, Britain and France declared their support for the Union cause; also on that day, Lincoln signed the Emancipation Act, freeing three million slaves.

The Battle of Antietam remains the single bloodiest day in American history.

'Mamie made me' tells the harrowing tale of Emmit Till, tortured and murdered in the town of Money. The details related are accurate. With astonishing bravery, Mamie put her son's mutilated corpse in an open-topped coffin for the world to see what white supremacists had done. His murderers were found not guilty in minutes, which spurred Rosa Parks to defy her old enemy, James Blake on the buses of Montgomery. Her act of defiance will be remembered as a tipping point in the struggle for civil rights.

'The Lost Season', a fictional account of a meeting between Captain Bouchard, who discovered the Rosetta Stone in Egypt, Marshal Junot, and Napoleon, deals with lost work by Antonio Vivaldi. The composer was, as is told in the story, frequently at odds with his patrons, and was banished to Piedmont.

'Get a message to my uncle' deals with the savage relationship between Cleopatra and her half-brother, Ptolemy. As guardian of their father's will, Julius Caesar intervened between them and set Cleopatra alone on the throne of Egypt.

'Recalled to life' juxtaposes the torture and murder of two girls at the hands of 'religious' zealots. Geillis Duncan was one of the first women to be accused, tortured and murdered during the North Berwick witch trials.

RECALLED TO LIFE

The last time I sat in the Memorial Garden, my parents were still alive. Today, the letters in black lacquer – *lest we forget* – and the red poppies mean more. The bronze sculpture of three first world war soldiers, heads bowed, arms reversed, I had never paid great attention to. The exotic plants of this Arts and Crafts area, contrasting with sombre copper lists of names of the fallen, should have had a calming effect, but did not.

My black bench had a brass plaque which I remembered from previous visits: 'For Teddy and Irene, who often sat here and enjoyed a fish supper.' I looked at the lists of the dead, picking out one name at random. Iain Farquharson, Lance Corporal, Kings Own Scottish Borderers, 1916. Imagining how Lance Corporal Farquharson might have died, I chafed the joint above the area of my right knee, not noticing a girl approaching.

'Are you in pain, lady?' she asked, her head tilted like a five-year-old. I was probably scowling as I looked at her, the scowl being my permanent expression. For all her childish manner and high-pitched voice, this person was at least sixteen, I decided. Although looking at her might invite conversation – something I had avoided since I came back from the hospital in Dusseldorf – her strangeness affected me. Plain white face, upturned nose, and anorexic build. Her clothes were quaint: dark brown dress, white apron, grey headscarf, like someone got up as a medieval servant for a fancy-dress party.

'I can help with the pain, lady. Come again tomorrow,' she said.

My knee clicked as I straightened it, causing the girl to start. 'You should let me help you, lady,' she said, taking my left hand, causing me to start. I detest uninvited physical contact as an invasion of privacy, yet this young woman persisted. 'I can give you something for your leg, and something for your heart, which is sore troubled.' Deep brown eyes and childish smile relieved the plainness of her face. I was so stunned by this waif's oddness, I did not even flinch when she placed her tiny hand on my chest, looking into my eyes.

'I am Julie Duncan,' she said, apparently by way of explanation, as though the name should mean something.

'Julie Duncan?' I repeated, my tone questioning. She shook her head and smiled again.

'Not Julie,' she said, repeating a name which sounded like Julie, but was not. She rolled her head from side to side, in a gesture which said it doesn't matter. 'I will gather plants tonight. If you come tomorrow, I can take your pain away.'

At that moment, the low sun shone between the corbeled Scottish Baronial roofs of the town, blinding me. After I rubbed my eyes, the girl was gone.

Back in my rented cottage, I typed, erased, re-typed the by-line *Kabul Airport*. Just as I had yesterday, and the day before, and for weeks before that. A futile routine. The Network was, of course, understanding at my failure to produce copy, but the editors would sometime run out of patience. A correspondent who does not correspond is an expensive luxury. I flipped down the Mac with nothing accomplished. 'No such thing as writer's block,' I told myself, 'just bloody cowardice.'

IN MY PARENTS' time, I used to walk the length of St. Baldred's Road in minutes, but the next day I took half an hour to hobble to the Gelateria. In a cross-grained mood, I ordered pistachio and caramel, a mediocre flavour. The coffee-coloured melt dribbled onto my hand by the time I reached the garden, where I parked my sticks against the nearest seat.

'Taxi next time, idiot; you're not fit to walk it,' I snarled, stubbing the half-finished cone on the end of my bench, the way Dad used to extinguish the full-strength Capstan that killed him.

'You should not punish yourself; it won't have been your fault.' She whispered so close to my ear that I felt her breath. Once more, I had not seen her arrive. That childish tilt of her head was the same, but something was different about her. As so often happens when an outsider makes an accurate personal assessment, I was furious with her familiar manner and gathered my sticks. Again, that tiny hand on my arm. From beneath her apron, she produced a small, brown, earthenware jug.

'It will work best if you let me put it on for you, lady,' she said. 'If you think it shame that people see beneath your skirts, no-one will notice. They never do.'

'Who's to blame, then?' I snapped, annoyed by this girl's presumption and my stupidity at listening to her babbling.

'A man,' she said with a shrug. 'Maybe more than one. It is ever men who hurt women.'

This situation had become surreal. Although, as a woman, I had struggled against prejudice in the cutthroat world of journalism, I am no feminist. Why was I listening to her? At that moment, a UPS delivery van pulled up at the ice-cream factory. The man in his brown overalls jumped down with an Amazon box. In slow motion, my companion lay down on the bench and curled into a foetal position, finally tucking her head under her arms. She made no sound, but her thin body rocked as if she were sobbing. Taking her arms, I sat her up, whispering what I thought was her name. She uncoiled. Without a word, she pointed to my knee and looked into my eyes, pleading; as in a spell, I nodded. Although I usually wore trousers, since I left the hospital, I had to wear spacious skirts. Though I expected an expression of horror when she discovered my prosthetic lower leg, she gave no sign, simply rubbing the contents of the jar onto the area above the plastic knee. I felt no immediate effect, yet the girl's ministrations were gentle. As she had said, although this was a busy square, no-one paid attention to our behaviour. It was like we did not exist.

As I thanked her, I realised what was different about her: her face, white yesterday, was deathly grey today. I pushed her headscarf back and shuddered. Deep red ridges, almost black, ran across her forehead. Congealed blood, in a line as thick as my thumb, round her head and into the line of her thin hair. Having spent months on the border between Pakistan and Afghanistan, I had seen many women tortured, but this was Scotland, for God's sake.

I spluttered at her.

'Men,' she said. 'The Baillie's men. Baillie Seaton. They put questions to me I could not answer. So, they thrawed me. If you return tomorrow, I will bring another jar.'

I put my hands to my face, trying to shut out the horrors

which followed me half around the world. When I uncovered my eyes, she was, as I expected, gone.

THE LAST GLIMMERS of the day's sun caused me to close the louvred blinds as I opened my Mac once more. Making no attempt to write up my notes from Kabul, I searched online instead. Often through that night, I found myself with my hands across my eyes, remembering the women, beaten, and humiliated by religious extremists. I saw a Saudi woman, stoned to death for suffering rape; I saw the body of a thirteen-year-old Indian girl, abducted from a bus, gang raped and beaten to death. And I saw little Julie Duncan, a Scottish child, tortured in her home town in the twenty-first century.

Since I found nothing on the internet to explain what Julie told me, I made do with noting phone numbers. Police, social work department and local press: I would call them all when I heard the girl's full story. Unable to sleep, I rose from my bed, poured myself a brandy, and thought over the last two days. The unreality of it convinced me that the balance of my mind had gone, after my horror in Kabul. Or else the drugs, given to me by an old school friend when I returned from Germany, were causing hallucinations. For a moment, the journalist part of my brain considered writing an exposé of Julie's abuser, when I discovered who he was. My better self, however, revolted at the prospect of exploiting this child's torment.

I woke mid-afternoon, lying across my desk, head on arms. The cocaine had helped me sleep, but now I was late. Expecting reality to return, assuming my visions of the previous days were drug induced, it shocked me to discover that Julie was there, seated on our bench. Beside her lay another jar, green earthenware this time. She neither rose nor smiled when I approached, but merely tilted her head in greeting.

'Is your pain eased, lady?' she asked, her voice croaking a little.

'It is better, Julie,' I answered, noticing to my horror her appearance had deteriorated overnight. The skin, like thinnest tissue paper, drew taught across her cheekbones; her eyes I could no longer see, as though they disappeared beneath the shadow of the cap she now wore.

'Drink the liquid ten drops at a time in mead or small beer,' she said in a voice as tiny as herself. Perhaps it was the guilty movement under her apron, wherein her arms remained out of view, or possibly I sensed a hidden horror. I reached for her hands and drew them out. Wrapped tight in stained linen cloths, her hands were obviously damaged. As I unwrapped the white-red cloth, she stopped me.

'Lady,' she whispered, 'you will be better if you tell me of your hurt.'

Staring at the bundled hands, guessing what lay within those blue-black bandages, I told of Benesh, a student of mathematics, who sat beside me on a bus to Herat. At noon, we were halted by the religious police, who inspected all the Muslim women. One of them held Benesh, while the other ripped the varnished nails from her fingers, ignoring my pleas and her screams. I went on with my story, telling of other horrors I had witnessed in the six months since I took the assignment. If the Network head suspected my presence as a western woman journalist would provoke incidents, to his shame, he was right. As the sun dipped once more, I unwrapped the girl's hands. Where there had been individual fingers, now there was a tangled mess of blackness, like the roots of a disinterred rose bush.

'Like your friend Benesh,' she smiled. For the first time

since I left the hospital, I cried. Then I told of the land mine which took my crew and my lower leg.

'Can you read and write?' she asked, head tilted once more. My impulse was to say, of course, until I realised the reason for the question: Julie could not. She raised her hands off her lap and whispered, 'Pilliwinks.' I did not understand the word, but assumed it was to be an instrument of torture. 'You should tell her story, lady. Your friend Benesh. People should know. Write it down.' She shook her head, causing the filthy cap she wore to dislodge. The action revealed a skull shorn of hair, the fresh, ugly scabs telling of the force used in the shearing. I was imploring her to return the next day, assuring her I would call the police to bring her torturers to account, when a Yamaha parked at the ice cream parlour roared into life. When I turned back from this new sudden distraction, she was gone.

I NEVER SAW JULIE AGAIN. My visit to the police proved fruitless. A WPC accompanied me twice to our bench, then offered a card with a number to call should evidence emerge. A week later, I decided to leave North Berwick. My own horrific experiences now merged with the torture of Julie Duncan. I was sick of the world, ashamed of my cowardice and of my impotence. My daily attempts to write were futile: all I saw when I looked at the keyboard were the bloodied hands of two innocent girls.

On the evening before I left, I returned for one last time to the Memorial Garden. The weather was changing, with a cold smirr in the air, which made ice cream unappealing. As I looked for Lance Corporal Iain Farquharson's name on the remembrance plaques, I heard the rustle of skirts. An elderly nun, dressed in a coarse brown habit. She almost smiled; I assume she recognised the disappointment in my face.

'She is gone,' she said. My facial response must have been anger or aggression, for she reached across, took my hands in hers and whispered 'Shh' with a familiar tilt of her head.

'Geillis Duncan, she is gone.'

For the first time, I heard the name clearly. 'Geillis?' I asked.

'They took her for a witch,' she said. When I tried to question her, she once more put a finger to her lips. 'Shh.'

'A servant girl from Tranent, she would give no consent to David Seaton, the Baillie's son. Accused she was of creating storms which prevented the king's return. Fingers crushed, hair removed, thrawed by the rope, they took her to Edinburgh. I spoke to her the night before she died. They probed her body lasciviously, which caused those wicked men excitement, for Geillis saw signs beneath their robes. A talent for healing the sick she had, which is why she came to you.'

'You are a nun from here, North Berwick?' I asked, the rain now falling steadily.

'Anchoress. Barbara Napiér, anchoress here in the toon. Forbidden to leave my cell, my anchor, but they came for me too. Geillis named me accomplice as the pain became too much; me, Agnes Sampson, others. They came for us all.'

Suddenly, the woman took my hand and pressed something hard and cold into my palm, a dark brown coin.

'This is all that Geillis earned through her healing of the sick. Tell her story, lady. Hers… and your friend's.'

OPENING MY COMPUTER, I placed the sixteenth century bawbee, with its piercing above the Scottish thistle, on my mouse mat. I began to type and tell the story of two sixteen-year-old girls. I had been paid to relate how the two, who might have been sisters, shared the same tortured experience at the hands of religious men.

'Separated by five hundred years, a girl from Tranent, Geillis Duncan, persecuted, tortured, burned to death at the start of the Scottish Witch Trials, November 1590; Benesh Ghulam, mathematics student, tortured, died of sepsis, Herat, November 2020.'

As I typed now, I no longer saw tangled black roots instead of fingers. I saw my fee, the life savings of the girl who healed me. Whose name I once thought was Julie.

I CAN PLAY SCARAMOUCHE

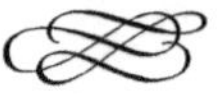

When I learned that my drama group was in rehearsal for an evening of extracts from Hollywood classic films, I spoke to our producer. Script writers were working on scenes from *Gone With The Wind*, *The Quiet Man*, and *Casablanca*; no doubt other suggestions would be accepted as the weeks went on. Many of the modern blockbusters were impractical. Any of the CGI dominated Oscar winners – *Star Wars*, *Lord of the Rings*, *Superman* – were beyond our budget and ingenuity to produce. Since our full ensemble consists of twenty at best – even including the arthritic ex-lollipop man and his schizoid wife – classics with big production numbers like *My Fair Lady* and *Ben Hur* were rejected.

'Well, it's a stretch, you see,' he said, when I pinned him down. 'We're almost certainly infringing copywrite as it is. We have to be careful to limit how wide we spread our net; we might get found out.'

This argument annoyed me. First, since he was pruning his roses, I was unsure if I had his full attention. Next, his point was absurd. Why include *Casablanca* but think *Scara-*

mouche would bring greater danger of discovery by copy-write inspectors? He was putting me off. I told him so. He put down the secateurs for a moment – either to listen to me or to pinch out some greenfly – and sat on the garden swing.

'Do you remember when we did *Singin' in the Rain*? We thought it was a brilliant choice. Fantastic comedy and terrific parts for principal men and women. But. How was it?'

'Rotten. A flop. We didn't even put on the second performance.'

'Right,' he said, using his heels to make the swing go. 'And why was that?'

'Because…' I said, feeling like a ventriloquist's dummy '… we had nobody that could dance.'

'Right again.' The swing was now more of a playground item than a garden relaxer. 'We cast the thing, thinking we would discover Gene Kelly and Donald O'Connor amongst our members. We didn't.'

'I remember. Cyril's performance of *Make 'em laugh* is still the talk of Tesco's, and Father O'Brien's wonky knee locked up during *Fit as a fiddle*. Pretty grim.'

At that, he got off the swing to return to his standard roses.

'Whoa! Wait a minute,' I cried. 'What's all that to do with *Scaramouche?*'

Waving his trowel in an aggressive manner, he advanced on me. Since he stood well over thirty centimetres taller, I was intimidated.

'What do people remember about *Scaramouche?* It's a swashbuckler. With the longest fencing sequence in all film history. Stewart Granger was a champion fencer; he worked with an Olympic medallist for six months before *Scaramouche* and *The Prisoner of Zenda*.' His advancing tactics now saw us nose to nose. 'And we don't have any fencers!'

I backed off, but only physically.

'I can play Scaramouche. I've watched the film hundreds of times. I've rehearsed all the moves. We could just do the scene from when he says: *You might turn your back on Scaramouche, my lord, but you won't ignore André Moreau.*'

'And then they fence,' he said, trowel now impaled deep into the turf. I nodded. 'For six and a half minutes?' I nodded again.

'And you think you're ready for a part of that importance?'

I squared up to him. 'I was outstanding in *The Mikado*. Everyone said so. I had a pivotal role. You claimed I was destined for bigger things.'

He bit his lip. I had him cornered.

'I've even got my own sword,' I said, producing it from my bag. Unfortunately, when I imitated Stewart Granger swishing through the greenery, I beheaded the begonias. Silence.

'All right, Scaramouche, who's going to play José Ferrer? The Marquis De Maynes?'

'You,' I replied, ready for a full-scale gloat. 'You did fencing at university.'

There was a silence, broken only by more begonias flopping off their stems. A long, dramatic sigh followed.

'Just a few things to mention here. One, I fenced for a single term. I was useless, and it was long before my hip replacement. Next, that's not a sword; it's a plastic souvenir from Edinburgh Castle. The pivotal part you played in *The Mikado* was the wee guy holding the Lord High Executioner's Axe. You'll be ready for bigger parts when you go to high school, maybe.'

'Dad!' I wailed.

'And finally, if you ever cut the heads off my flowers again, I'll skelp your backside!'

MAMIE MADE ME

Mamie was the bravest woman I ever knew or heard of. One of my cellmates thought I was brave. The others – women of the streets, judging by their fishnets and low-cut tops – said I was a dumbass.

'Whydah do it for, girl? You knowed they was gonna stick you in here.'

'What? Too tired to get off that skinny ass?'

Well, I wasn't brave, and I wasn't tired. Some folks have said it was because I was just tired that I did it. But I wasn't tired. The only tired I was: I was tired of giving in. But Mamie, Mamie was brave.

She showed how one brave woman can try to change the world; can help cure the sickness that has lasted in this country since the end of the war. It was supposed to have ended in 1865, after Lee surrendered. But that war ain't over; it's just that the battlefields are different. Some people, a lot braver than me, keep trying to bring it to an end. Mamie was one of them. She believed things could change.

To understand how strong her faith was, you have to put yourself in her place when she first saw the body. The horror of what she thought, what came into her mind then, I can't imagine, thank the Lord. The knowledge that your boy was crying for his momma, that she might make it stop, but she wasn't there and couldn't hear him: what mother could bear that?

She sent him off to relatives, just days before, from her home in Chicago. That city, whatever its problems, is not in the deep south, like Money, Mississippi. They use the Jim Crow laws there. In Chicago's South Side, he could go on buses with white boys, go to school with white boys, go to the ballpark with white boys. Nothing unusual. But the boy had heard stories of life in the Delta Counties and wanted to see for himself. Mamie warned him about life 'Down South.' You had to mind your manners around white people. Don't expect fair treatment or respect, 'cause you won't get it.

Smart, fun, friendly and beautiful: he was a good boy. His smile could light up a street at night. When he was eleven, he stood up to his stepfather when he threatened Mamie. Brave even then. His stutter would have held back other kids, but not him. His street crowd looked up to him, like he was always thinking up tricks to play and fun to have. So, Mamie let him go to spend some time with Uncle Mose, who she knew was careful.

The day he left, the Eighteenth of August, was the last Mamie saw her boy alive. Just three days after he arrived in Money, he and some others went to play checkers on the sidewalk in town. Two in the afternoon, a couple of the boys ran across the street to buy sticks of gum. The owner's wife, black-haired, slim, and pretty, served them. She was used to serving 'negroes' since the local sharecroppers were the store's most frequent customers. What happened next, she lied about: lied to her husband, lied to her brother, lied in court. She would admit in later years that she made it up that Mamie's son put his arm around her.

All the world knows what happened next. After coming back from a trip to Texas, her husband and brother listened to her story. Arming themselves, they drove in a pickup to the shack where Uncle Mose lived and took the boy. Although his uncle offered them money, they took the child anyway. They dragged him to a barn in Drew and what they did to him nobody wants to hear. Witnesses heard him cry out, 'Help me, Mama,' and 'Please don't do it again!' But they did anyway. Finally, when they were done with him, they shot him in the head and threw him in the Tallahatchie River.

It's the next bit that makes Mamie a hero, an inspiration for all who need the strength to carry the fight to the oppressors. What she saw when they pulled her boy from the river can't be described. He had been in the water for three days and his body was bloated. Even without that, he would have been impossible to identify. What they did to that child was the work of demons. What would always stay in Mamie's mind was that his right eye was not where it ought to have been. Now you and me, we would have wanted poor Emmett to be buried without fuss, keep him out of the sight of his friends and family. But that's not what Mamie did. She ordered a glass-topped coffin and put her boy's mutilated body in it, had it shipped back to Chicago and left in church for all to see. This is what the brutality of ignorance and bigotry does.

And they came in their thousands. Black people, white people, men, women, newspapermen, priests, deacons, minsters, and politicians to see what segregation, intolerance, and white supremacists were guilty of. I came too. My husband and I both worked for the National Association for the Advancement of Colored People. I saw what they did to that boy, and I knew I would not take it anymore. We had had enough of being treated like animals, like we didn't belong in the white man's world. There was nothing else in my life mattered from that moment.

I HAD MET HIM BEFORE, of course. Blake. Twelve years before. I know because I made an entry in my diary: 'Never riding again with that man driving.' That was August '43. During the other war. That time I had paid my fare, as usual, then he told me to go back and re-enter the bus using the rear door. James F. Blake, his badge said. You have to understand what we put up with on buses in Alabama: we had to sit behind a sign that said 'Coloreds'. We had to pay our fare at the door, then leave the bus and re-enter through the back door. We couldn't sit across the aisle from white people. So, it wasn't unusual to be told to get off and get on at the back. But what James F. Blake did was wait till I got off and then drive away, leaving me to walk. In the time I took to get off and go to the back door, Blake drove off.

And here he was again.

The segregation of buses in Montgomery, Alabama, was almost legal. There were laws – Jim Crow laws – that said we couldn't sit beside white people; we couldn't eat in restaurants with white people; we couldn't go to school with white people. Because court cases challenged the segregation of schools, that was changing. And the white folks in the south didn't like it one bit. It took me three tries to register to vote, and even then, I had to run a gauntlet of spit and hate to do it. I suppose buses have always represented the evil of segregation to me since I was a child myself. I remember with bitterness travelling to Pine Level School when I was eight. When I say travelling, I mean walking. Only the white kids caught school buses, only the white kids travelled in style.

So, when I boarded the bus after work on the First of December, it was only four days after seeing Emmett's mutilated corpse. I had just heard an hour before that they set his killers free. Sixty-five minutes it took the jury. 'If we hadn't stopped for pop, it wouldn't have taken that long,' one juror said. When the driver came up to me, that's what I was thinking about. I didn't even notice other whites had filled up the seats in front. Now, the way these drivers worked the law, they could take the sign saying 'Coloreds' and move it when they wanted. And here he came, the same name badge, the same smug, arrogant, contempt-filled smile on the face of James F. Blake.

'Get up and move to the back, you negroes. There's white folks needin' them seats,' he said to the four of us sitting there. The three others got up.

'Why don't you make it light on yourself and move,' he said, smiling, eyes staring, enjoying his white power.

'I believe I will not,' I said, smiling back. He reached towards me, as though he would drag me, I swear. But with a bus full of passengers, he took a step back.

'Why don't you stand up, else I'll call the police,' said Blake.

'I don't believe I will,' I said.

While waiting for my arrest, two thoughts occupied me. The last thing on my mind, as I told the women in jail, was what was going to happen to me. By that time, I realized, as thousands of us did – black and white – that the fight had to be carried to people like James F. Blake. We knew we would have to endure the spit, the hate messages, the dead cats left on the porch, the burned-out churches, like the three here in Alabama. But every fight has a cost, and I was ready for it. But first, I thought about Mamie, who had defied the racists, showing the world what they had done to her son.

And I thought about the face of little Emmett Till, whose right eye was not where it should have been.

The Montgomery police were not known for their gentle

manner when dealing with protesters, but the sergeant carrying out my arrest was more amused than aggressive.

'Why didn't ya just stand, Beulah? The law's the law,' he said.

'I'm fed up being pushed around. Arrest me all you want, but I won't accept it anymore, not once,' I said. 'And my name is not Beulah nor Jemima. It's Rosa. Rosa Louise McCauley Parks.'

THE WEE TRAIN ROBBERY

*R*onnie McKerrell is a sleekit slug; it could be him. Anna, the fifty-year-old Goth, is capable of anything. McMeekin inhabits the planet Neptune. What about Ben 'n' Bill, the Tweedle Dum and Tweedle Dee from *Alice in Wonderland*? Grandad Baillie alone is beyond suspicion; he's just not strong enough or quick enough to be a robber.

If we hadn't all watched last year's *Great Model Railway Challenge*, this would not have happened. We would have pottered along as ever, three nights a week, all obsessive geeks together in the converted Fort Elizabeth station. As clubhouses go, despite the lack of heating, this one accommodates our shared mania well. In recent years, we have picked up several impressive pieces of Railwayana: tin signs advertising Player's Navy Cut and Guinness, as well as levers saved from the skip when Troon South was closed. Best by a mile, though, a genuine footplate from The Flying Scotsman. If you watch *Bargain Hunt,* you'll know that tin Railwayana adverts are worth a bob or two. That's because the internet's second biggest searches are model railway related. (Most searches are for pornography, which I imagine also interests McKerrell.)

Anna laughed as she explained how she drove the rest of her family nuts binge watching *The Railway Challenge*, to the exclusion of *Eastenders* and *Strictly*. Naturally, when we heard about a programme featuring teams of modelling-maniacs building a layout in three days, competing in a grand final, we joined the binge-brigade. All fine and dandy, you might think. We discussed how idiotic the team from Falkirk had been trying to build the Hogwarts Express viaduct at Glenfinnan in the three-day timescale.

Normal clubs have committees and meetings thereof; our meetings are mêlées. As nominal president, you would expect me to preside, but that would presume some kind of democratic organisation. Scratch any model railway fanatic, and you will find a psychotic narcissist. It was Anna, six feet tall, with a giraffe neck, and orange streaks in her treacle hair, who wrote off to the TV company. She suggested we would make interesting contestants for the next series. Imagine a nest of black widow spiders, injected with bile, on a bad day. That does not come close to the lava of venom and blasphemy that erupted as our group tried to reach a consensus. Eventually, with only the strongest left standing, we decided to fill in an application form, with two-thirds abstaining.

Then, the real fun began: picking a team of five. With the chance to appear on telly, even Grandad Baillie drew metaphorical blood, his false teeth inflicting psychological damage on the rest. The matter might never have been resolved if a power surge had not rendered the clubhouse uninhabitable for two weeks. (I put it down to Ben 'n' Bill overloading the circuits by wiring up their version of Operation Overlord. Their layout featured the invasion of Normandy in 1944 – complete with tanks, landing craft and a squadron of Spitfires. This to an already overloaded set of multi-blocks. It did not impress the Fire Brigade or Scottish Power.)

The upshot was a meeting in Gerald's mansion in Bridge of Weir. This semi-castle in Scottish Baronial style fair impressed the rest of us. The problem was Gerald's main rooms, the tower apartments, being circular and of modest floorspace, could only hold half a dozen people per room. Since twelve turned up, this meant two separate meetings, one floor above the other. That the total group, including Gerald, made up thirteen might have given notice of an ominous lack of good fortune. There was certainly a lack of goodwill.

In the top turret, I attempted to preside over the power players, while Gerald shepherded the rest of the flock into the room below. We all knew the format of the competition: a team of five, equipped with our own trains and two pre-built items of scenery, with three days to build a railway layout on a literary theme. Since Gerald has always been obsessively shy, he had no wish to take part. Indeed, he comes to the club armed with his Rottweiler and stereo headphones to isolate himself. When McKerrell objected to the presence of the hound, the said dog explained through bared teeth and throaty growl that its presence was essential to McKerrell's continued health,. The objector was muzzled.

I spelled out how a team should be made up. We needed a whizz at electrics, at least one competent track layer, a computer expert to run the programmes on my laptop, and two model makers. Imagine a U.N. conference with Iraq, Iran, Israel, France, U.S. and Syria. Add Donald Trump, an Al-Quaeda chief, and Katy Hopkins, and you have the composition and tenor of our group. As club president, I put my name forward for consideration. After sixty minutes' character assassination by the others, I pointed out that I had the best trains, including a Basset Lowke live steam locomotive for which I had paid £10,000. They considered this a clinching argument. Bobby reasoned he was the only electronics expert. While this was certainly true, his massive bulk caused sharing a layout with him cramped and damp. McKerrell made the point: it would be difficult to share the space with him. ('You're a big, fat, sweaty bastard.') Nonetheless, we accepted Bobby as number two.

When Anna popped down to the room below, she was voted out, simply because she was Anna. On her return, she declared the other group had chosen *Macbeth* as the literary theme. McKerrell slimed her by pointing out that the first trains did not run until many centuries after Macduff accounted for said Macbeth.

'No worries,' Anna responded. 'It's supposed to be a twentieth-century version.' It fell to me to explain to Anna that she would not be on the team, whereupon she let out a scream which emasculated all the men present. They reinstated Anna after she quoted a curse from the Scottish play. (I have to say, from the looks she gave me and the others in the room, she did not whole-heartedly withdraw that curse. Events would prove this to be so.) Even the most selfish contenders admitted that 'The Doc' Varinder Singh, our orthopaedic surgeon, was the best model-maker in the group. We returned him unopposed, leaving a single vacant slot. An invasion from below filled the place to overflowing, added to the turmoil, but reduced the breathable air by half. Like a cartoon from *The Beano,* the place was nothing but arms, legs, heads, and fury.

Enter the elephant into the room. Unbeknownst to the rest of us, Gustavus Coull, our non-speaking modeller, had made his way to Bridge of Weir. Announcing his presence with his usual bass growl, he glared around, holding an iMac over his head. As the meeting settled, he forced his way to the circular table. No-one had ever heard the man speak; he communicated through a series of guttural grunts, when he wished to communicate at all, which was seldom. Gustavus was the reincarnation of Karl Marx. Grizzly grey-black hair, worn long, frizzed past his mouth to an enormous beard. If anyone doubted the resemblance was deliberate, the Cossack fur hat he wore sported the hammer and sickle. Although everyone – even Anna and McKerrell – was afraid of 'Gusty', he never intruded on our lives to any degree. He spent all his time at the club on his own layout representing Kremlin Square and St.Basil's Cathedral.

Yet here he was, offering to join in a communal activity. When he laid his Mac on the table, the screen displayed a new German train controller, the most sophisticated, elaborate method of running a layout via a computer. I had heard of this marvel but did not possess the technical ability to use its software.

We had chosen out team. No McKerrell, no Ben 'n' Bill, no Grandad Baillie, no McMeekin. Leaving out these five might have seemed the logical decision, but – coupled with the idiocy of choosing the most cursed piece of literature ever written – would lead to our downfall. Once Scottish Power had restored our electrics, we returned with a determination to prepare for our appearance on the box. Was everyone fully committed? Certainly. Was I confident of success? Not a chance. There was so much resentment crackling round the clubhouse, we didn't really need Scottish Power's input.

I designed a three-level layout, trying somehow to incorporate a *Macbeth* theme. There are different sizes of models, called gauges. The smallest – 'N' gauge – uses trains about eight centimetres long. The most common – 'OO' gauge – has engines from ten to fifteen centimetres. My Bassett Lowke beauty, being live steam, involves liquid, so needs another kind of rail altogether. Imagine it like this: a teeny train chugging along the top, carrying Macbeth to his missus; the middle track would see him meet the witches at Waverley Station; my live steam in the foreground would end with good old Macduff chopping off the baddie's head.

The clubhouse was full on the first week of preparation, including the drooling Doberman and Grandad Baillie's grandson, Wee Chic, complete with his Iron Man backpack. Work on the mock-up began that night, with everything going smoothly, as normal. In other words, Gothic Anna giving a brilliant impression of Lady Macbeth by cursing McKerrell, the Doberman nibbling Ben 'n' Bill's nuts, and Wee Chic weeing in the corner. As I was on the point of closing up, Comrade Coull growled. For the first time, he used words.

'Some bastard's stole mah Bachmann Norfolk Southern.' Gusty's top loco, an expensive German 'N' gauge train, was missing. Like one of the Poirot films, everyone stared at everyone else in the room. I suggested we search all the dozens of boxes which litter every model railway clubhouse. Nothing. To my mind, everybody present was a suspect. It occurred to me that those who had not been selected for the team might, in a fit of jealousy, sabotage our efforts. Once again, I looked around the room. Gustavus was right: some bastard stole his Bachmann Norfolk Southern. Even the Doberman was a suspect.

If Gusty thought that our Sunday meeting, being on the sabbath, might constrain the villain to return his loco, he was wrong. Although the atmosphere was strained, the rest of the members got on with our plan, while Karl Marx stood, eyes blazing, gazing at the empty section of track where his train should have been.

Worse was to come. On the following Monday, Ben 'n' Bill's OO gauge Flying Scotsman vanished. By now, everyone turned up to the meetings, since absence might suggest guilt. I kept my prized asset locked in my briefcase. While we tried to figure out how the layout would work with substitute engines, there were murmured suggestions we call off our participation in *The Great Model Railway Challenge.* Gustavus was more forthright: 'You thievin' bastards should scrap the club.'

The straw which finally broke this camel's spine came during the next meeting. As I checked on The Doc's design for his scratch-built Glamis Castle, McKerrell slithered up and nudged me. 'And then there were none,' he sneered, inclining his head to my now open briefcase. I lost it. Literally and metaphorically. Although not given to hysteria, I went to pieces at the theft of my Basset Lowke Engine, accusing everyone present: McKerrell (of course), the mad Goth, Ben 'n' Bill, even Grandad Baillie and the waif with him. I stopped short of suggesting the huge dug had eaten my train, though the drooling bastard was capable of it. But I did resign on the spot.

THE BITTERNESS of a woman betrayed knows no bounds. By the end of the week, I was searching the internet looking for wax dolls and accompanying hatpins. During one particular sulk, I searched eBay for Basset Lowke engines. I knew they were now out of my price range, but I searched anyway. Because they are among the best locos in the world, they are always pricy. Real steam versions cost big numbers. Like a pathetic wean staring in an expensive toy shop window, I surfed for two hours. After returning from the loo, I saw it. 'Basset Lowke live steam locomotive, pre-owned but in great condition, offers start at £50.'

'£50?' I cried. 'It looks just like mine. It is mine! There's the bit on the tender where my weathering went wrong.

Who is the thieving bastard?' I wailed, blood pressure volcanic. I looked at the seller's information. 'I know that email address. The thieving old bastard!'

HERE'S THE THING, though. You can't just turn up at someone's house and accuse them of theft. Or take a baseball bat and splatter them to bits. Well, you can, but you end up in chokey. So, being subtle, I thought of a plan.

'Madame President,' said the old man, smiling. Having welcomed me when I arrived uninvited, he offered me a cup of coffee. As per my plan, I invited myself to see his layout. Puzzled, he was, but ask any model railway buff to see their layout and watch their dust. As he creaked his way up to his attic, I sensed fear in his slowing steps. He was onto me.

When we got there, however, there was nothing other than a standard eight by four figure-of-eight Hornby starter kit. No 'N gauge trains, no sign of The Flying Scotsman, and certainly no Bassett Lowke. As I made a show of admiring the miserable layout, Wee Chic rumbled up the stairs, chattering about a Hewlett Packard something or other. Didn't sound like a train, though. When he saw me, his expression changed. Like a startled rabbit before you roadkill it, he froze. His eyes went to a clock on the wall. I had seen this kind of Railwayana before: a huge clockface shaped like a train depot, with a miniature track running under the hands. And there, on the tiny track, was Gusty Coull's 'N' gauge Norfolk Southern, rotating on the hour and half hour.

Grandad Baillie, plainly innocent in the matter, spotted it at the same time as me, mouth falling open. We both looked at the station at the top of the clock, where a three-dimensional version of The Scot took the place of the painted one on the front. Gramps could say nothing, so shocked at the implication of all this. When the child culprit smiled like a Cheshire Cat at me, the dam burst.

'Right, you thievin' little shit. Where is my Basset Lowke?' I screamed, fingers itching to embrace his skinny neck.

'I need more money to buy a computer,' he whined. 'I put it on eBay.'

And then: 'Want to bid for it?'

THE LOST SEASON

Often, after an engagement involving artillery, a heavy mist mingles with the stink of ordnance, especially in late evening as the dew rises. The smell is bitter, the taste in the mouth acrid. And there's the sweet scent of blood lying overall. Today's inconclusive battle in a nameless bog in Piedmont would find no place in the history of this endless war. Just another minor action, with no advantage gained or lost, resulting in three hundred casualties. As I waited outside the Marshal's tent, my boots sank into the ooze. The soil in this country is like that: a sickly yellow even when not sodden. I took the letter from my satchel, trying to decide if I should present it to the man I had come to meet: Marshal Junot, commanding the Eighth Corps of Napoleon's Army here in Piedmont.

Standing in my way, Auguste Daxx, *L'Exécuteur*. Junot's aide-de-camp, fanatically loyal to the emperor. His massive chest showed the stars and medals won serving Junot and Napoleon. His dark blue uniform, even in this gloom, gorgeous, glittering with gold braid and aiguillettes. If today's action had exhausted him, he did not show it; his movements were brisk, angular, and straight from the military academy. Daxx, a member of The Old Guard. Before me stood the perfect image of the French soldier, fit for any recruiting poster. For all his fierce reputation, he was courteous in his refusal. Often, when soldiers of the Old Guard see a captain in my uniform – the bottle green of an engineer – they find courtesy difficult. The disdain fighting veterans feel for those not facing canister and musket ball is understandable but unjust. The wounds to my shoulder and neck from an English dragoon in Egypt testify to the dangers I have faced in the service of the emperor. I squelched further into the mud as Daxx hesitated. The metal box, bulky and balanced awkwardly on my sabretache hip, grew heavier as I waited for him to be convinced.

'The Marshal is much concerned with important matters,' Daxx said. 'Dispatches arrived from Paris this afternoon, Captain…?'

'Bouchard. Pierre François Bouchard. Captain of engineers. An historian, an archaeologist.'

If I believed this introduction would help me gain entry, I was wrong. The words were hardly out of my mouth when Daxx smiled, shook his head, then laughed. I assumed that, in the aftermath of a bloody encounter with the Austrian forces, declaring that as an archaeologist, I had a right to the marshal's attention sounded foolish. It forced me to produce the letter.

'I have this carte for the Marshal.' On the thick outer paper, the words *Marshal Jean-Andoche Junot, Duc d'Abrantès, Commandant du Huitième Corps, au service de Empereur Napoléon Bonaparte.*

Then I loosed my cannon shell. 'It is signed by Le Comte Fouché.'

Even a man like Daxx, brave beyond measure, flinched at the mention of that name. Fouché, head of the secret police.

Responsible for a thousand deaths at the guillotine: many aristos, some merely his own enemies. I tried to read the changing expressions on the aide's face. Not fear, perhaps, but suspicion, hatred probably, contempt certainly. Then he squared his shoulders, jutted his massive beard, and whispered to himself, 'En avant, the Old Guard.'

'One moment, captain,' he said, the edge in his voice like the steel of his sabre.

When I entered, Marshal Junot gestured for me to sit on the solitary stool. Jean-Andoche Junot, commander of the Eighth Corps, hero of Toulon and Austerlitz. What struck me was the paleness of his face in the flickering candle light. And the exhaustion in those dark eyes. Unlike Daxx, his uniform – the blue-black of a marshal of France – showed signs of today's battle. The red epaulettes did not lie straight; splatters of mud were evident on his breeches and boots. Only the white gloves he always wore were clean, doubtless replaced within the last hour. He poured a cup of wine and slid it across the campaign chest, which served as a table. On the two occasions I had seen Junot before, he was fastidious in uniform, despite being constantly on the march. Not today.

'I have heard of you, Captain Bouchard?' he asked, holding Fouché's letter, yet unopened. 'But not, I think, as a spy working for the chief of police. Are you a spy?' Even his voice, cultured as befitting the lawyer he had been, showed stress, cracking now and then; the sentences were stilted.

'No, sir,' I answered. 'I am an archaeologist.' I laid the precious box on the sodden ground. Black tin, hinges rusted, heavy with the paper contents. Junot narrowed his eyes. Realising I had not asked his permission to put my burden down, I apologised. He inclined his head.

'Explain,' said Junot, after taking a sip of the sour wine.

'Since the conquest of Egypt, sir, the emperor wishes to

be known as a man of science. Any discoveries which might increase his reputation in that respect are to be trumpeted abroad.'

'Especially in England,' Marshal Junot nodded. 'Perfidious Albion brought low by the great man of science, Napoleon Bonaparte. Hence Fouché's note, giving me orders, no doubt. But I have heard your name, captain. You discovered something in Egypt. A tomb, was it? It was reported in *Le Moniteur*. Mentioned in dispatches, too.'

'A slab of granite, sir. Important because it conveys the same message in three languages. In time, we will discover how to translate the writings of ancient Egypt. I found it at Rachid, or Rosetta, as we know it.'

'I presume you have a reason for this visit tonight,' Junot said. Despite his hospitality, his terse tone and fierce stare told me I had limited time in his presence.

'Today, sir, in the ruins of a nearby monastery, my men discovered this box. I have looked inside. I believe it is of importance.'

Junot wiped the dust from his brow and hair. As a result, he emptied the wine from his cup, having spoiled it with grit. Since he was known to be a man of uncertain temper, I waited for a dismissal. He poured us both more wine. As he picked up reports from his desk, I had little of his attention, I felt.

'And this thing of importance… military? Scientific?'

'Music, sir,' I answered, waiting again for an explosion. Instead, he put his left hand on his brow and spread the fingers, the gesture of a tired man. For some moments, he inhaled deeply before covering his eyes with both hands. The smell of the cheap tallow dips caused me to splutter.

'Captain Bouchard. I await word of the Austrians advancing on my right, towards us here at Piedmont. Prussia is assembling a force twice the strength of this army. When

Alexander finally makes up his mind, we may have to invade Russia, and that will be the end of our dreams. You wish me to listen to your tale of a tin box which contains music? And this is important?'

I did not answer. In this mood, Junot would dismiss anything I might have said, I felt. Placing his long fingers on his neck, he rubbed the throbbing veins in his throat, then closed his eyes and breathed deeply again. He laughed.

'You see before you, captain, a man with the weight of an empire on his shoulders,' he said. 'But the distraction you will provide may help me think more clearly. Proceed with your tale of important music, Captain Bouchard.'

Realising that I must make my case before the marshal's patience wore out, I began. I explained the monastery here had provided sanctuary for those fleeing Italy a century before. The marshal inhaled deeply, then picked up another report. A clear signal.

'In the box, there are hundreds of pages of manuscript, with musical notation in the same hand. Equally important, I found a journal, by the same writer. The man was a composer.' I asked to read from the book; Junot, eyes closed, nodded. Just as I began, a third person, a soldier, entered the tent and stood in the shadows behind me. The marshal, looking up, rose from his stool before the voice from behind whispered 'assieds-toi'. The atmosphere had changed. Convinced that my time here was limited, I raced through my story.

The journal, I explained, was written by an Italian musician and one-time priest. He had been excused from his parish duties to compose music, which appeared to have met with success. The man, however, was of a rebellious nature. As a teacher in a hospital for the poor of Venice, he had produced famous girls' choirs. Unfortunately, he lost patience with his employers and threatened violence to a mayor, as well as his bishop. At this point, Junot smiled.

'I approve of this composer. A sans-culotte in temperament. A Jacobin, possibly.' There came a sound from behind: a disapproving grunt.

'Go on,' said Junot, looking past me to the figure behind me. I went on. I continued by saying the man had been sent into exile here at the Benedictine monastery of Piedmont. Hence the reason we found his work.

'Do we know of him, this musician?' Junot asked.

'I believe his name is Antonio Lucio Vivaldi. He may at one time have been celebrated, but if, as seems to be the case, he was sent into exile, his patrons will have seen that his work was rejected, discarded. Yet his masterpiece, *The Four Seasons*, is a work of genius, and well-remembered. And what we have in this manuscript is a piece called *The Fifth Season*. He conceived the idea that there was a fifth season, which encompassed the others. He says: 'The Fifth Season is a time when the other four come together: the turning of the leaves and their budding again, the heat of the summer, shimmering from the tiled roofs of Venice to the ice forming on my solitary window. It is the mists rising from the valleys to disperse as they reach the heat and height of the Alps. And all at once, one piece of music celebrates the season we have lost sight of.'

'What do you make of this Lost Season idea? An exiled man's desperate fancy. Had he lost his mind?' Junot asked.

'Or maybe the vision of a musical genius, trying to express the splendour of God's creation,' I said.

The soldier behind me moved into the light, towards Junot, who stood.

'The aides outside tell me you are Bouchard, the man of science who discovered the granite stone of Rosetta,' the other man said, peering at me.

'Yes, sir,' I answered. Since the newcomer's battle-stained blue coat carried no insignia, I did not know how to address him. There was nothing to distinguish this man. Heavily built, of florid complexion, with thinning hair: nothing of distinction at all. Apart from the blazing blue-grey eyes. He whispered, leaning towards me. More threatening by far than any hysterical roar.

'The Republic of France has no place for God, his creation, or his disgraced priests. The French Empire recognises only one supreme figure, that of the Emperor Napoleon Bonaparte. Take the box back, put it where you found it, and concern yourself with earthly matters, Captain Bouchard. Find a tomb, or a slab of granite.'

I stood up, stirred to stupidity. 'The music, sir, whatever it celebrates, whoever composed it, deserves to be heard, surely?'

'You would defy your emperor, captain? Junot, the men have their cooking fires lit?'

'Yes, emperor,' snapped Junot, with a click of his heels. The short, undistinguished man seized the manuscript from my hands and thrust it at the marshal.

'Add this to the flames. Now, Captain Bouchard, The Lost Season is truly lost.'

BEAUTICIANS SHOULDN'T GET PLASTERED

I don't like this part of the city. It's the snob capital of Glasgow. The inhabitants pronounce it Newton *Meerns* and deny that they are Glaswegian. I had an appointment at a beauty shop here early on Tuesday morning. I therefore expected 'Nails, Hair and Skin-Glo' to be pretentious and full of blue-rinsed matrons wearing Burberry skirts and Hermès scarves. Except if they were having their hair re-coloured, in which case, I was sure their clothes would be protected by Armani coveralls.

Beauty salons are also places which cause one of my hang-ups to stir. The images in my mind come from my playing Frenchie in the school's production of *Grease*. Within the pink scenic flats designed by the art department, I had been surrounded by a dozen of my classmates decked out in pink shrouds and wearing white, fluffy wigs. My boyfriend of the moment, Fraser McLarty, serenaded me with *Beauty School Dropout*. The experience scarred me for life: the stage crew had not tested the pulley lifting spotty McLarty at the end of the song. The resulting fall caused me a broken collarbone, and Fraser to drop instantly from boy tenor to the deepest bass. Love was dead.

I was surprised and relieved when I did arrive at my destination. I found a subdued and tasteful establishment set off Maxwelton Drive, between 'Pooches 'n' Poodles' and the Co-op Funeral Director's Emporium. I wondered whether the blue-rinse ladies would have noticed the difference if they had strayed into the doggie shop for their grooming. And vice versa. I suppose poodles like perms, though not sky-blue ones.

'Nails, Hair and Skin-Glo' had an aura of pleasing gentility, with less pink on the exterior than I expected. The shop's name was displayed in a modest rose gold, as was the name of the proprietor, *Bettina Mulvenney.* A colourful exhibition of Gatineau products dominated the window, mirrored by several display cases within.

My workmate Sheila, already in the parlour, introduced me to the owner, Bettina Mulvenney. Never having heard of anyone called Bettina, I assumed her actual name was the less exotic Betty. This lady was thirty-five, I guessed, with an elfin face, slim-without-being-anorexic figure, and welcoming manner. Just the sort to put anxious sixty-year-olds at their ease before assaulting their hair and skin. Her blue eyes sparkled, giving the impression that she was alert, focussed and bright. First impressions can be misleading. Insisting that we call her Tina – *it's what my friends and clients call me* – she offered us both coffee.

'It's Colombian, so quite strong,' she said, 'and not to everyone's taste.' I offered to help her with the percolator, seeing that a heavy plaster hampered her right wrist and hand. I was impressed with the whiteness of the stookie. Another on my list of things to hate are plasters with pink writing and rude messages – *hope you get a stiffie* – or which have been inked the shade of a Glasgow football team. I suspected that Tina may have used shoe whitener to maintain the condition of hers.

'Can't wait to have rid of the bloody thing,' she said. 'I've been using a knitting needle to scratch at the itching. I'll bet it'll look like I've been self-harming when they take it off. That'll be tomorrow if I can get away. Sweetener?'

At this point, she waved a bottle of Jaffa Cake flavoured gin at me. When I declined, she sloshed a generous triple helping into her own mug. As she audibly sipped her coffee, I noticed the wording on the mug: 'Tina the Brow Lady – Live to Pluck.' Pretending to sip the Colombian firewater, I rejected this offer of an alcoholic 'sweetener.'

'So, how did you come by the stookie?' I said, peering through the toxic steam of my own coffee cup. I have only ever once tasted gin when my friends and I decided to become sophisticated. I remember thinking that's what perfume would taste like, so I supposed Jaffa Cake Flavoured Gin would taste like satsuma Chanel.

'Well, that's when I got suspicious,' she said, trying to replace her mug in her workstation's cupholder. 'I'm a serious biker, you know.' She leaned forward to stress her point by miming a cyclist slaloming down a track, holding the handlebars of an imaginary bike.

'Cycling is my thing. I have a KGS Tier 3 Custom Bike. Don't even ask what that cost. I am good at it.' At her second attempt, she managed to pick up her mug and sipped again as she warmed to her description. 'I win competitions: off-road, long-haul, mountain ascent. I am a superb, fantastic cyclist.' On the words superb and fantastic, I pulled my head away to avoid spit as Tina sprayed her 's' sounds at me. By now, I was convinced she was more than a little tight. Those first impressions. 'I have the bike serviced every couple of months. With special attention to the brakes and gears. So how come the brakes failed coming down the Lothian Stretch? Unless…' At this point she went into a mime routine which could have been many things but was supposed to be someone sabotaging her bike with a spanner.

I could see where this was going. 'Unless someone tampered with your bike? Someone who had it in for you?' Tina slumped back in her chair and nodded.

'When did you first meet Dolores Labelle?' I said, steering the conversation in the direction I needed it to go.

'Dolores Labelle, my arse', she said. Once again, the 's' sound produced a squirt of coffee-coloured spit. 'Senga Mitchell, she was at school. The name is as fake as the screaming blonde curls and the sticky-out falsies. Thirty-two B cup, if that. Flat-chested as a snake.' To stress her point, Tina wiggled herself in her chair, hoping her own boobs spoke for themselves. Dolly Parton, however, she was not.

'But that's the weird thing, how she showed up,' she went on. 'Apparently what happens is Mum and Dad are at their allotment behind Rouken Glen Park, when this man comes up to them and says he knows them. They remember him from the school PTA. So, after Dad's usual lecture about the dangers of slug pellets, the guy asks about me and what I am doing. To cut a long story short, when he hears about this place, he remarks what a coincidence it is, because his daughter has just finished a course of Beauty Therapy and is looking for a start in a salon.

'Well now, I ask you: set up or what? That wee bitch Senga had figured it all out before sending her parents to meet Maw and Paw. By the way, do you know what they called her at school? Senga the Slapper! She got battered once a week for getting off with somebody else's guy. I couldn't care less about Donnie Armstrong, if he'd such rotten taste to get off with that wee madam. And he had blackheads on his nose.'

When I prompted her for more details, she reeled back to the counter and refreshed her Colombian with gin.

'She turned up here a couple of months back, all cheesy smiles and giggles,' Tina went on, warming to her subject. 'She had one of these cheap white nylon smockeralls, with the name *Dolly* above her left boob. 'Dolly', Jesus! Said my dad had promised her dad I would give her a month's trial. It turns out that Dad said nothing of the kind. But I didn't know that then, so I had to agree. I binned the Dolly-embroidery and gave her one of my salon's capes. It was too long. And a bit grubby and well-used. Just like her.'

'So, you did give her a start in here?' I asked. Tina wobbled up from her chair and found the gin bottle again. She must have seen my look.

'I'm not an alkie, you know, if that's what you're thinking. I can stop any time I want.' She put the bottle down again. She stood leaning on the counter as she continued her character assassination of Senga the Slapper.

'The first week was just about okay,' she said, 'I suppose. She was weaselling herself in though. I told her she could sweep up the hair, hoover up the bits of nail, check deliveries, and tidy up. All good, responsible jobs. The trouble started when I came back late from walking my dog and found her doing Mrs. Templeton's brows. Brows are my speciality. *Tina the Brow Lady*, it says so on my Facebook page.'

'And did she make a hash of it?' I asked. 'Mrs. Templeton's brows? Right eyebrow higher than the left?'

'It was okay, for an amateur, I suppose,' Tina went on. 'But I don't do amateur – Tina the Brow Lady! I didn't let it pass. I closed the shop for half an hour and gave her laldy.

Oh, she turned on the phony, squirting tears as fake as her tits. I told her she could work up to nails, maybe in six months. But that Saturday, that very Saturday, I came off the bike. Think that was a coincidence? I knew right away it was her. Bet she'd been at home, sticking cocktail sticks into a wax model of me. Then she came up with the idea to fix my brakes.'

'What makes you so sure the brakes were...' I started, re-enacting her mime, before she talked over the top of me. By now, bubbles of spit and coffee were forming in both corners of her mouth.

'Ligaments and Christ knows what all!' she galloped on. 'Six weeks with this stookie on, and not able to work. No hair, no facials, and no brows. I had no choice. Close the salon? How could I pay the rent here? So, I had to let Madam Mim loose on my customers. I tried to keep an eye on things, but the cuddly, pink-fluffy act fooled them all. *Can I have Dolly do my nails today? Is it all right if Dolly cuts my hair? I'd like Dolly to do my brows, Tina, if that's all right?* The wee bitch conned them all. One time, she was waxing Councillor Mitchell's upper lip, and I caught her looking at me with that smug Minnie Mouse expression, shrugging her shoulders – what there are of them – and then winking at me.'

Tina realised her booze was finished and reached for a metal skewer. I had no idea why this lethal object was in a beauty salon, but I got up from my chair and took a step backwards. She then inserted it between her arm and the plaster and scratched.

'So, that brought matters to a head, did it?' I said, recovering my dignity and chair.

'Oh, no, that's not it,' she went on. 'No, no, no, no, no. Not nearly. It was yesterday. I was on a bus heading for Mum and Dad's. I can't drive with this on, so I was on the top deck of the number forty-nine when it stopped at Mearns Cross.

Next to Smith's. I suppose because it was a Sunday, and because of Covid lockdown, most of the shops were shut. That's why I noticed her. There she was, a shopfitter van outside, watching this guy putting the finishing touches to her shop window. Her own bloody shop! *Dolly's Hair and Beauty.* There she stood, admiring her salon, arm round that spotty bastard Donnie Armstrong. And then Mrs. Templeton parked her Merc and ran over to her, no doubt promising to be her very first customer.'

'So, you had enough,' I said, my voice full of sympathy. 'What happened today?'

'I decided last night to let bygones be. Then I thought: Will I fuck! So, I set up a demonstration for her in the salon. There's a new hair restore device from Italy. It's supposed to stimulate the follicles. I was in early, assembling it, rigging it up in one of the hair styling chairs, the tubular metal ones, you know? Metal conducts electric wires well, doesn't it?'

'And that's when you killed her?' I said, returning to my dispassionate questioning.

'Well, I convinced her, since I would get this stookie off tomorrow, I would be able to get back to work. I said I was sure my old customers would be loyal. Then I wished her luck with her own salon. I explained she might like to try the latest in hair styling equipment. Particularly good for balding women. Like Councillor Mitchell.

'And that's when you killed her?' I repeated.

'It was quite humane, really,' she said.

'But you rigged up an electric chair, like in Texas?' I asked, persisting.

'She didn't half sizzle for a while when I switched it on. She lasted for about five minutes. I didn't actually time her. Still, she did stop giggling early on, though it's hard to tell between giggling and sizzling,' she said in a fit of girlish laughter as she relished the memory.

She went back to her coffee cup, drained the last dregs, and put it down with an air of satisfaction.

'Are you going to arrest me now, Sergeant?' she asked.

I nodded. 'But we'll let you get your stookie off tomorrow.'

THE QUEEN OF VAN DIEMEN'S LAND

For a moment, as the young man stared at my neckline, I thought he was interested in my bosom. Realising that his gaze was focussed on the heavy gold pendant round my neck, I sighed. 'Those days are long in the past,' I mumbled.

'Your pardon, ma'am? I asked when you came by the title Queen of Van Diemen's Land,' he said, shifting position on the wing back leather chair. An eager young reporter, hoping to make his name, only interested in the story and not my bust.

'And your editor thought I might give you an honest reply? Knowing *The Melbourne Argus* has only a limited understanding of the truth?'

The boy blinked behind his silver-rimmed glasses, at once pleading and disappointed.

'Ask your questions,' I said, smiling at this callow reporter's lack of guile. 'I'll answer. But you'll let me see your article for approval before going into print.' He nodded and flipped open his pad. Was I really about to recount my story, having guarded my past for so long? My wicked sense of humour – only one of my wicked traits – urged me to do so.

'You came first from England, ma'am, is that right?'

'Islay, off the west coast of Scotland. And yes, those rumours are true: I arrived on *SS Southern Cross,* docking at MacQuarrie Harbour in '48. You're bound to ask why I was sentenced to Penal Deportation from Islay. Because the readers of *The Argus* want to know how I became a queen. Me, a common convict. Well, I was no common convict. Catherine MacDuffie has never been a common anything. On Islay, I was a *besom richt oota hell,* according to the minister and dominie. *There's no' a man oan the island'll pit up wi' yon red-haired bitch fae purgatory,* my own uncle said. So, to keep me away from trouble, the family put me to work on the peats and seaweed carts. They need peat for the Lagavulin.'

The young man frowned, having missed much of what I had just said, it being in my native tongue.

'Lagavulin, Mister Chan, is the whisky of the world. Would you take a dram?' Another frown.

'Cutting peats takes a tushcar, wi' a strong arm and back. A spade with a long blade, a tushcar. But I'd a way with men at ceilidhs, in those days. In spite of what the uncle said, men liked my red hair. One Sunday, when God-fearing islanders were at the kirk, I'd the peat beds to myself. Up comes Mary McFadden, a flat-chested, mackerel-faced bitch, and she calls at me.

'You're a hoor an' a thief,' she calls. 'Ye've stole Donald McDonald, who was promised to me.'

'She was a lying wee midgie. Donald McDonald was a loon, but he was not blind. I threatened her with my tushcar but settled for throwing half a peat. Well, the peat stains, and she stood there like a blackamoor. The next day I'm lifted by the baillie, taken across on the ferry to Inveraray Courthouse and sentenced to eight days in the jail. Eight days at mending the herring nets; eight days with one pint of soup and a hand of bread; eight days of fighting off the men who wanted to enjoy my red hair.

'One month after leaving the jail, they arrested me again. Mary McFadden was found head down in the peat bed. McTavish the Sergeant said he'd never seen a body wi' a square heid. Someone had pounded Mary McFadden's head with a shovel, till it was the shape of a half peat. They blamed me, but they had no proof. My tushcar, well, they searched for it, but it had gone missing. They inspected my clothes for blood, but I'd a new dress and boots from Aunt Maeve that just died. After another three weeks in Inveraray Jail, they sent me to trial. In the end, the jury found me Not Proven, but before I left the dock, Lord Henry Cochrane, the judge, found me in contempt for what he'd seen in court. He'd a report from Sergeant McTavish of my shameless conduct at the ceilidhs, and from the minister at my breaking the sabbath. Cochrane sentenced me to Penal Deportation to Van Diemen's Land.'

'You must have been furious at that. Deportation, because the judge did not like you? Deported for minor offences like that?' Chan asked, looking up from his scribbled notes. I took to this young man. He seemed genuine in his outrage at my treatment. *You'll not last long in this business*, I thought. Sitting back, I waved my hands about me.

'What do you see here, young man? Bronze statues, gold ashtrays, silver bracelets. These earrings are pearls, this ring, a diamond. If I had rested on Islay, I might still be cutting the peats. Or worse, married to that loon Donald McDonald.'

My secretary interrupted us, bringing reports for my signature. As I read through the documents, Helen fluttered her eyes at the smart young man across from me until I caught her.

'Three o'clock, Helen Dawkins, time for my glass.' Chastened by my tone, Helen, a fellow Vandemonian, fled, though not before flashing half a wink at Chan. On her return, I poured myself a whisky, having given the reporter another chance to enjoy the finest drink on any continent. I lit a cigarillo.

'I developed a taste for these while in The Female Factory, ten miles from Melbourne. We bribed the warders with them.' When I offered him one, he accepted, possibly because he felt refusing all hospitality put his interview at risk.

'The Lagavulin prevents staining to the teeth. And my teeth have ever been one of my attractions.'

I believe my smile captivated him, as it has with so many men. Despite the differences in age and status, I enjoyed the effect I was having on Mister Chan. Perhaps those days were not so long in the past. I relented, releasing him from my spell long enough for him to return to his story.

'Was your imprisonment in The Female Factory at MacQuarrie as bad as…' He searched his notes.

'Inveraray Jail? It was different. It was all women there, so that stopped me being pestered by other convicts. But the warders — mainly men – I'd to fight them off. Most were afraid of me. Remember, I'd a strong arm and back, from cutting the peats. The food was better, the work the same; the lice, mosquitos, and snakes, much worse.'

'And you earned your Ticket of Leave by serving your sentence?' he asked, trying his best to smoke his cigarillo. I laughed.

'Not in the usual way, no. No common prisoner, remember? MacQuarrie was the easier of the landing grounds for minor rascals like me. Port Arthur, the other port, was reserved for real criminals: rapists, murderers, thieves. After I had six months of making sackcloth, one of the guards from Port Arthur was transferred to our factory. Bentley. A vicious man, even the warders at Arthur had enough of. So, they let him loose on the women at Melbourne's Female Factory. You can imagine what happened. Most of the women let him do what he wanted. Afraid, do you see? Nothing stopped him, and some women suffered beatings, bleedings…. I'll not say more; you couldn't print it. One woman, she could read. She told us a story about a boy in a poorhouse that asked for more food. We did the same. Drew lots to decide who should take care of him, Bentley. We all knew I was the only one there that could sort him, though.

'I did not get the chance. One night, there was this terrible screaming from the warder's barracks. Warder Bentley had been 'sorted'. The tendons on the back of his legs had been sliced, then his head struck several times by one of the irons we used to make sack cloth. His head had been flattened.'

Young Mister Chan choked. Either from cigarillo smoke or from what he had just heard.

'Like the woman on the island?'

'Mister Chan! What are you suggesting? The cases were nothing like each other. The woman on the island died; Mister Bentley did not. Certainly, he could not walk, and his head was flatter than before…' To calm the reporter's coughing, I left my chair, patted him on the back, then rested my hand on his shoulder, long enough for him to smell my scent.

'For the second time in my life, they made me suspect of a crime, with not a bit of evidence. I knew what was coming, though. The other women would have given me up if I didn't confess. Your editor won't print this either, *The Argus* being a good Christian newspaper. The warders would force the women to talk. They'd get babies on them. The women warders – most of them on licence – were worse. They'd hold the women down while the men did it to us. They did

The Barrelling to me, too. A long, steep stony road, just outside the factory. They put me in the barrel, nailed the lid shut, then rolled it down. It's hard to breathe inside a barrel. Especially when your bones are breaking. Ten, twenty times, they did it. They said they'd put a rat in with me the next day if I didn't confess, and then they would hang me. And Van Diemen's rats are as big as dogs.

'For the first time since I was cutting the peats on Islay, someone helped me. A wombat of a man, Tommy Peters. He opened the barrel and took me out that night. For all he was queer-looking, he saved my life. Not for charity, you understand. He liked my red hair; wanted to enjoy it. If he took me away in his cart, he said, he'd set me up as an indentured servant 'to look after his needs.' So, under the load of hemp he'd bought at the factory, Tommy concealed Prisoner 827B and made his way north, to the highlands.'

It might have been inhaling Spanish cigarillos turned him green, or maybe the unprintable bits of my story caused it, but young Mister Chan, close to vomiting, needed help to stagger into the garden. I half-carried him. Helen, quite happy with putting her arms round the well-dressed stranger, beamed as she did so. I let her enjoy the moment before having her bring a glass of lemonade to revive him.

'The Lagavulin would work better,' I said, as I straightened him up in the wicker chair. The gardens in Melbourne are a wonder, and mine is the best of them. The sound of the fountain, the flaming colours of the silky oak and giant candles trees, and the cooling breeze from the lake, brought him round.

'I've already mentioned it: there's bits you won't get to print.' I resisted the urge to pat his head, but the young man was aware of me. To clear his mind and concentrate on his assignment, he removed the glasses, wiped his eyes, then accepted his notebook and pencil from Helen, who had followed us outside.

'And yet you survived, flourished even,' he said, his voice a croak.

'It's not a fairy story. Tommy Peters was no handsome prince, and Ballarat no magic kingdom. After I recovered my strength, he wanted his needs looked after. He was a wee man, however, and his needs were easily looked after. A preacher in that lawless place took an interest in me, taught me to read and write, loaned me books on different subjects, including business, making money, investments. For all he was a man of God, he liked my red hair.

'Tommy Peters worked at the Yuille Station. A family of Scottish brothers, the Yuilles, had an eye for money. They sold Peters – it was me they dealt with – a flock of sheep. In two years, I ran the biggest sheep farm at Ballarat Station. Business, Mister Chan, I got very good at. The railways were just starting up, the men needed clothes and food, and *The Ballarat Sheep Company* was formed. Tommy's share satisfied him. But not me. Things might have gone on that way, comfortable but no more, until the Second of August 1851.'

Chan sat up at the mention of that date. Pushing his glasses back on his nose, he leaned forward.

'I know about that. They say the moonlight caught a glimmer, and that's how he made the strike.'

I laughed, leaning forward to pat the young man's knee.

'If that's what you want to write, you go ahead. He'd been drinking at Harvey Bent's Saloon, couldn't find a latrine, and pished in the stream beside our hut. And where he was splashing, there it was. A nugget, the size of my thumb, the start of the first Victorian Gold Strike. Because of a drunken wombat's waters.'

'That nugget – a piece of Australian history – they say it's in a museum in Melbourne,' Chan said, looking up from his scribbles.

'Do they?' I asked, fingering the gold piece round my neck. 'The place soon became known as Specimen Gully. It's still there but played out now. You know the rest. In those days, you could walk along the bed of a stream and pick up two or three pounds of gold in a week. Within a year, Tommy Peters was the richest man in Victoria.'

'And, as his wife, you must have been the richest woman.'

I laughed again. 'Me? I was an indentured servant. I put away some pieces for myself in a bank, but otherwise, no. Tommy drank and gambled, while I saw the chances for real money. This was the richest place on earth, then. We argued, Mister Peters and me. I wanted to invest in what I knew was going to make money; he wanted to spend it. Funny that: pissing away the wealth he got by pissing in the first place. The Yuille Brothers saw it the same as me. Lifting some of Tommy's shares, I sold them, and with the Yuilles set up *The Phoenix Foundry Steam Locomotive Company*.'

'I'm sorry, ma'am, but when you say lifted...?'

I lit another cigarillo.

'I was a partner, though a junior one, in my own right. Next year, *The Melbourne and Hobson's Bay Railway Company* was founded. Now I became the major stockholder. Tommy Peters, still wealthy, thought I was using his money and neglecting his needs. There were always rumours about me. A lot of businessmen in Victoria – like most men – admired my red hair.

'By now, surface panning was played out; deep cast mining was needed. Tommy Peters, checking whether his investments were working, inspected some of the mines. One night, he just disappeared. Likely it was the collapse of a side shaft; they never found the body.'

'You seem to bring bad luck to the men around you,

ma'am,' the reporter commented.

'I don't believe in luck. You make your own. And plenty of others made their fortune through me.'

Realising I was troubling the young man, I leaned forward, formed a bridge of my fingers, and smiled with my eyes. Hoping I might reassure him, I whispered as though I were taking him into my confidence.

'Leon… that's your name, isn't it? Leon, times were bad here, tough. People died. New settlers, convicts, ex-convicts. Accidents, riots, disasters. It's not like now. Melbourne – all Victoria – is civilized. There's law. Courts, police, justice. A lot has changed in ten, twenty years. Transportation is finished.'

'You had something to do with all that, though, didn't you? That's why they call you the queen of Van Diemen's Land. You helped during the riots. With….'

'With your people, the Chinese? During the rush, we were pulling out two tons of gold a week. That brought an influx of immigrants, and not convict labour this time. Italians, Germans, Swiss, but most of all Chinese. Sure, I saw the trouble coming. People like to hate incomers, bully them, kill them. In Scotland, it was the Irish, same as America. In Victoria, there were three sides: the Vandemonians like me, the free settlers, and the Chinese.'

Perhaps something struck a note with Mister Chan. He delved into his satchel and produced newspaper cuttings.

'I didn't come without doing my research, ma'am. Head-lines from *The Geelong Advertiser*: **Chinese workers massa-cred in Canvas Town. And this: Government to introduce White Australia Act.**'

I shook my head before calling for a further drink. By the time Helen supplied me with my dram –trying to flirt with my young friend in passing – he had drawn another news-paper from his bag.

'But this is what brought me here,' he said. 'From my own paper. **Surprise intervention in race riots. Local Widow Catherine MacDuffie-Peters elected to State Senate. Brings about immediate truce.'**

I could not stop myself from laughing. Throwing my head back, I let out an unladylike guffaw.

'An hour ago, I told you about *The Argus* and its idea of truth. Three sentences there, three lies. If I were the coarse besom I was in Islay, I'd tell you where to put that paper. But, since I'm the Queen of… I'll just tell you what really happened.' Sipping another drop of Lagavulin to stifle my laughter, I adjusted my dress, flicked at my hair, and began.

'Since I have never been married, I cannot be a widow. James Scobie was… Let's say he admired my red hair. James was a lucky striker. He'd staked a claim north of Ballarat and came up lucky. His partner registered the claim to the mine, then died of food poisoning. Remember, I told you about the size of rats here? No doubt that's why Mister Scobie bought all that arsenic. People died. What he did with his wealth, James Scobie, was buy people. He bribed saloon keepers, brothel-holders, crooked mine owners. He was useful to me in building up my own businesses: sheep, railroads, property.'

I noticed Chan had stopped scribbling; instead, he scratched the deep frown, furrowing his brow. As I studied him, I felt his unhappiness. Not the persecution of his people, I thought, but me.

'Mister Chan,' I said, a schoolmistress tone in my voice. 'You came here today to hear a story, one that other reporters couldn't get. But more than that: you came to visit royalty, ready to be impressed, prepared to sit before the throne of a legendary queen. I'm none of those, and I'd be ashamed to be so. I saw it in your eyes the minute you came in. You have the look of an idealist, and now you are disappointed in what you've found. I'm rich, powerful, and ruthless. And when I finish my telling, you can decide if it's worth exposing a legend.'

'It's just that I remember the James Scobie Case. Again, it was reported in *The Argus*.'

'Of course it was.'

He produced another copy from his satchel and held up the headline.

Prominent Businessman, Syndicate Manager James Scobie slain by Vandemonian Policeman. Bentley to hang.

'*The Argus* at least got one thing right: calling James Scobie a syndicate manager,' I said. 'That was the words they used for being the boss of local extortion and blackmail gangs. Whatever you now think of me, Leon, I have never been a crook. I knew James was involved in that kind of business, but since I lived in Melbourne, I ignored it. Until my maid Libby, an aboriginal girl of fifteen, broke down once night and pleaded for my help with her family. The gangs in Ballarat and surrounding towns were selling cheap whisky and brandy to the Aborigines, putting them in debt, then buying their children for prostitution. Libby's sister was twelve. I went back to Ballarat. I found James Scobie in the Eureka Hotel, along with his bodyguard. After I sent the other man from the room, I accused him of forcing girls to become…. He didn't deny it, and we argued.'

'When you say argued, though, ma'am, was it words, or….?'

'James Scobie was a big man. Taller and heavier than me. And drunk. The rest of the story will be in the report. He attacked me. At the sound of fighting, his bodyguard ran in and got involved. There was a struggle, and he killed Scobie, hitting him on the head with a miner's shovel. One blow.'

'The newspaper report says the man pleaded his innocence. His defence lawyer pointed out that Bentley was disabled with a heavy limp, and because of his disfigured face, he didn't see well. He blamed Scobie's wife in common law. You.'

'There is nothing common about me,' I said, lighting another cigarillo. I inhaled deeply before sipping my drink.

'And this Bentley, this was the same Guard Bentley, from MacQuarrie's Factory?'

I gave the young man my best smile and nodded.

'Strange coincidence, wasn't it? At the trial, it was the word of an ugly bully, known around the area as a brutal enforcer for the gangs, against mine. A wealthy, respected and – if I might say so – beautiful woman. They jury believed me. They executed Bentley. Another coincidence, as well: Scobie's head smashed flat, like Bentley's.'

As I thought about the hanging, I paused.

'And how do you feel about all that?' Chan asked. For the first time, I resented the judgemental tone in his voice.

'We'll end the interview now,' I said, standing. I called for Helen to show the reporter out. As he gathered his papers, I looked again at this naïve boy, trying to make his way in a business for which he was not suited.

'Sit down,' I said, the schoolmistress back. 'Whatever you suspect about 'all that', I saw that Libby's sister was freed, and a lot of other children, too. When I turned over Scobie's records to the police, more than one criminal gang was broken up. They're back, of course, this being the richest territory in the country.'

'But you went home after that, I understand,' he said. Once again, I laughed.

'I went back to Van Diemen's Land, if that's what you mean. Safer there, fewer criminal gangs looking for vengeance. There I was, the wealthiest woman in Australia, with powerful friends all over the country. Van Diemen's Land, a wilderness. Wild and beautiful, like Scotland, with its mountains and lochs. But I saw opportunities. Roads, railways, farming, all waiting for development, and I had the money to do it.'

'By now, locals were calling the island Tasmania. Transportation was over. An area to the south, already established by fishing communities, was called Greater Hobart. I worked from there, alongside two women, both ex-convicts. Elizabeth Macarthur, with my financial help, set up *The Merino Wool Company*. I had met Mary Reibey in The Female Factory, another of the women who drew lots about Guard Bentley. She was forced to marry a guard, Günter Heinrich, to get her Ticket of Leave. Between us, we had the idea of setting up a bank.'

Chan, like so many naïve men, could not conceal his emotions or lack of understanding.

'What I don't understand, ma'am, like a lot of my readers, is how so many women from Port Arthur and MacQuarrie had such influence. Not only in Van Diemen's Land, or Victoria, but across the whole of Australia.'

'It's no mystery, Leon. Think about it. Into a country where a small proportion of the inhabitants are female, comes ship after ship of women with unique skills. People like me: farming and management of the land. Some of those transported were bookkeepers, writers, and businesswomen. New skills, new ideas, and the determination to escape from all sorts of chains. Mary Reibey and I returned to Melbourne using our substantial capital, and even more substantial business brains, to set up *The First Colonial Bank*.'

'But something happened as you returned?'

'The shipwreck,' I answered. 'Yes. The Bass Strait can be a dangerous crossing in winter. Mary and I, as well as her husband, Günter, were aboard the SS. *Tasman*, when it foundered close to land. Mary and I swam ashore.'

'And Günter?'

'He fell from the rocks as we landed.'

'He has not… what I mean, he didn't have injuries to his head?'

'No, and I don't know what you suggest by that, young man. No, he died during that shipwreck.' I gave him my warmest smile. 'Of course, when he fell, he did land on his head.'

Leon was swallowing hard now.

'The rest, well, you already know that Mary and I, along with two others, became board members of the bank. Later, during the race riots, I used my tact and diplomacy to settle the matter, giving the Chinese settlers what rights they now have.'

'By diplomacy you mean…?'

'I used the state police to threaten them with deportation to London, Manchester, Glasgow. That settled the dispute.'

The young man closed his notebook, gathered his notes, and, for the first time, smiled.

'Ma'am, I am not sure how much you have told me is fact, how much is legend, how much you have teased me with. And I don't know how to write all this up.'

I almost winked at him.

'One more question, if I may?'

I inclined my head in agreement.

'That gold piece. It is not a nugget, is it?'

'It was a nugget. The first one. I had it fashioned into this.' I held it towards him. 'It represents a spade, with a long blade, used for cutting the peats. A tushcar. I had it made. The original served me well over the years.'

I watched as he blanched, leaning backwards.

'You don't have to worry, young man. My peat cutting days are over. I am, after all, The Queen of Van Diemen's Land.'

THREE CIGARS, NINETY-FIVE PHOTOGRAPHS

When I stare at the three cigars now, they look like fat twigs, having lost their moisture. Once they were a cheap brand for low ranked soldiers. Keinert's smokes, five cents apiece. The three most important cigars in my country's history.

When I replace them in the aged trunk, I remember how important its contents are, and promise myself to send it to Pinkerton's vault. A Union Army Cavalryman's trunk, the wood almost black now, the same colour as the heavy straps and locks. This I found at the scene of the First Battle of Bull Run. The owner's name stencilled along the top: *H.L. Schuyler, Co.G. 6th PA. INF.* I neither met nor heard of this man, who served with Company G of the Sixth Pennsylvanian Infantry, but I use his trunk for my treasures. My most valued of these is The Butler Medal, known as The Colored Troops Medal. Since I am the only white woman to win this – for action in The Battle of Combahee Ferry – it is a unique award. The person who should have won the medal was the greatest hero I ever knew, Harriet Tubman. My other medals are in the trunk, including that awarded by

Congress. And my sabre is there too, with the personal inscription on the blade, and *Tiffany & Co* on the hilt.

Yet these cigars, which could have saved this country three years of slaughter and did not, still changed the history of the world.

THE MISSION BEGAN in the Chicago office of Pinkerton's Detective Agency, years before I gained any of those treasures. In the spring of 1862, this building was unofficially a branch of the US Secret Service. My boss, Allan Pinkerton, apologised for sending for me, as he did when the job meant serious risk of death. Speaking in the Glasgow accent he lapsed into when worried, he explained that 'a senior official' had asked for a spy to be sent to intercept 'Bobby Lee.' His Confederate Army of Northern Virginia was advancing into Union territory.

'Don't like askin' this, lassie, ah surely don't. Union General George McClellan is movin' so slow the president fears he might be pushed back tae Washington. They're callin' him 'Gorgeous George', his troops, and don't they love him! He got them better food, better clothin,' better pay – nae wonder. But whit's the point o' building a model bloody Army o' the Potomac if ye don't bloody use it! Yer pardon, lassie, fer the speech.'

Since I had never heard Allan Pinkerton swear, his 'bloodies' surprised me.

'I have tae ask it, though. Lee's army is movin' through the Shenandoah Valley intae West Virginia. If we find oot for sure where he's headed, maybe we can force Gorgeous George tae fight him, an' use the bloody army he was given. It'll mean disguise for ye again. But yer the best spy I have, Astrid.'

I hate the word 'spy'. It described what I did, but I hate the word, anyway. My father, an honourable policeman, would have baulked at it; my mother would have scolded me in Swedish. I agreed to Allan's request. Before leaving the office, I scribbled a note of some people to be contacted, as well as items I would need. My plan was forming.

Squinting at my list, he made little comment other than to ask if everyone in Sweden thought *in queer order*.

MY FIRST CALL was to The Bijou Theatre, and to Hannah. As owner and producer of Chicago's best small theatre, this tiny woman had already created several disguises for me. Although she often pleaded with me to remain with her and resume my career as an actress, Hannah was ever a source of costume ideas for my guises.

'Do you know anything about the people you hope to deceive? And anything of these… professions you wish to join? Apart from that one, of course,' she said, pointing at my list.

I shook my head. 'But, with the country in chaos, with every family having sons, fathers, brothers killing each other, a confident manner and a very little knowledge gets you through. After I've seen Cornet, I'll start here,' I said, indicating my notes.

'And you'll need to become a man for this?'

'Of course,' I answered. 'Whoever heard of a woman scientist?'

CORNET LIVERMORE'S HUT, on the edge of Ashtown, the grimiest area of Chicago, was part shooting gallery and part arsenal. Like Hannah and Allan Pinkerton, this close friend had grown used to my thinking *in queer order*. Despite his initial scorn when I joined Pinkerton's as an agent, this former British soldier was a staunch ally. He was also a rich source of information on a hundred obscure subjects. Including the one I asked him about now.

'I should have known that the only person in this city to express an interest in the photographic process would be the handsome Swedish strumpet. Drink?'

'If you have aquavit, yes. Otherwise, enjoy the gin yourself.'

Carefully pouring the clear spirit into his British Soldier's Mead tankard, he offered me a stool while adjusting his mask. The scarring to his face – an explanation for which he never provided – meant that this once handsome soldier wore a metal pyramid where his nose should have been. With a black-red scar running from above his right brow to his lower left jaw, Cornet's was a fearsome appearance, matched by his abrasive temper, and deadly skill with weapons. Without going into detail, I explained the journey I must undertake, the stops I had to make, and my final objective.

'Anyone else asked this of themselves, I'd say they were mad. For you, just another assignment the Scotch Fox has given you. So, we'll spend a day or two on the difference between the daguerreotype, the ambrotype and the albumen print Brady uses. A further day to remind me how useless you are with guns, before making up for that with better weapons. Then we'll be off.'

'*We* will go nowhere, Cornet Livermore. You have business to attend here while I travel west.'

Wiping his mouth on the once scarlet British uniform he still wore, he smiled, put his feet on the table, and belched.

'The only business I have in Chicago would result in my killing a senator's son. Which he badly needs, I might say. Otherwise, I am at the disposal of an uppity foreign female who, needing my scientific skills, will agree to my joining her on this adventure.'

Despite my protests, I was glad of Cornet's offer. His knowledge of arcane matters was unparalleled; his accuracy with any weapon he chose was the best I had ever seen, and I had spent the last two years among the military. Of greatest importance to me now was that he had worked with codes. This had involved correspondence with Samuel Morse, whose handwriting I wished Cornet to forge.

'You are not telling me over much, madam,' he muttered, as he scribed the letter for me.

'I have learned that the less I tell others, the chance of my being discovered also decreases.'

'And that includes me?'

'It includes Allan Pinkerton, President Abraham Lincoln, and Cornet Joshua Livermore.' I checked the wording:

Mathew Brady
Willard Hotel
Washington
August 18th, 1862

MISTER BRADY,

Since we last met, I learn that you have developed your use of the Albumin Print. I also believe you employ some of my former students in a travelling studio, recording the brutality of this war. Although my principal area of activity continues to be the telegraphy, I maintain an interest in all forms of art and photographic systems.

I bring to your attention, therefore, a young protégé of mine, Timothy O'Sullivan, who hails from your own country. I would be grateful if you would employ him in your war project, that he may, on his return, instruct me in the use of this moveable studio.

· · ·

YOURS WITH THE GREATEST RESPECT,
    Samuel F. B. Morse.

BEFORE SETTING OUT TO WASHINGTON, I explained the reason for the game I was playing. Not only to satisfy Cornet's curiosity but also because my plan included asking him to take my place at a crucial moment.

'I intend to discover the whereabouts and intentions of Lee's Army of Northern Virginia. I know they were last seen heading for the Blue Ridge Mountains. They camped at Chancellorsville, preparing for an invasion of the north. That much I already know. The photographer Brady sends his assistants to record the aftermath of battles. They are well known and accepted by both sides. If I were among those assistants, I could travel freely, with no questions asked by either Union or Confederate soldiers. This would allow me to determine where McClellan might take the Rebels by surprise. After that, I have a theatrical performance to give.'

'And that is all you will tell me?' My smile gave him his answer. 'And Allan Pinkerton does not know this?'

'Nor Abraham Lincoln.'

'I'm duly honoured, Swedish strumpet. Now, to get into Brady's team, you could offer a scientific system he may not know about his printing. But it's complicated. Do you suppose a blonde actress from Stockholm might grasp it?'

'The Swedish actress from Jönköping will struggle but has enough patience learn that *and* endure insolent English ex-soldiers. Proceed.'

I WAS BORN to be an actress. The very first time I stood on the stage of Hannah's theatre, I knew it. There is no thrill like playing a part. With that familiar sense of excitement, I knocked at room 12 A, a private suite in The Willard Hotel, Washington. A middle-aged man, wearing a green visor, with shirt sleeves rolled past the elbow, opened the door, tutted, and asked my business with Mister Brady. As he prepared to close the door in my face, I thrust the note of introduction through the gap, requesting an interview.

'Letter from Breese Morse, Mathew. Want to read it?' the man shouted. Following a mumbled reply, I was admitted and told to sit down. Though I was a frequent visitor to The Willard – the most political building in Washington apart from the White House – I had never seen a suite turned into a laboratory before.

Mathew Brady, dressed in a three-piece tweed suit, carrying bundles of letters, emerged from what had once been a bedroom. His brown, curled hair showed tinges of grey; an exuberant moustache and beard accentuated the cheekbones and nose. On stage, he would have been a director's ideal tragic hero. Removing his gold-rimmed spectacles, he began cleaning them with a napkin from a table laid for breakfast.

'Hmm? Who are you? Read me the letter, Roche,' he said, perching on the back of a chaise longue. After the first man had done so, Brady leaned towards me, face almost touching mine. 'Why should I take you in, boy? They need waiters here at The Willard. You've the appearance of one.'

'I can help you improve your printing, Mister Brady.'

One of my favourite characters, both onstage and as a spy, was Molly, the washerwoman from Killarney. By lowering her tone, sporting a cheap, chequered suit, and wearing my blonde hair tight beneath a checked cap, I became the Timothy O'Sullivan Brady now scowled at.

'Indeed?' he said, replacing his glasses. 'How so?'

'Once you have coated your cotton paper in egg white and salt, then added the silver nitrate, you position the paper against your negative. Finishing the process in a bath of sodium thiosulfate, you fix the exposure,'

He swivelled round, sitting now on the arm of my chair. I was unsure whether he suspected my disguise or if he was short-sighted. If his intention was to intimidate me, it worked.

'This much I already know, laddie, though I am surprised a youngster like you knows so much.'

'I can only remind you of Mister Morse's letter, sir,' I said, pulling back an inch or two.

'And this improvement you speak of?'

'Using gold toning, before the fixing process, improves the colour and stabilises against fading.' This speech, coached by Cornet, was almost my total knowledge of the Albumin Print. I had, however, learned how to prepare the toning solution of which I spoke. I hoped this might make me a useful addition to Brady's group.

He sat up, opened a humidor, lit a cigar, and paced. Muttering to himself, he crossed the floor over and over. At one point, the man called Roche tried to interrupt, but was brushed aside. Like a manic character in a melodrama, he suddenly leapt back to my chair, almost brushing his nose against mine.

'Can you make it? This gold toning solution, can you make it?' I nodded. 'Show me,' he yelled, dragging me by the wrist into another room. With lamps shaded by green cloths, this was what was called a darkened room. The furniture which typified The Willard suite's second bedroom had been moved. Bed, bedding, wardrobe, and double settle were all stacked against the mirror wall, with no dust sheet to protect them from the dust and debris the photographic might send into the air. Three well used trestle tables, certainly not originally from this expensive hotel, stood central, with trays, bottles and jars occupying every inch of their surface. The smell of chemicals was acrid and irritated the eyes.

Using the milky grey liquid supplied by Cornet, I mixed a minute portion of gold filings to produce the gold toner both Cornet and now Brady thought would provide results. Brady disappeared into another room, then reappeared with a negative, moving like a whirlwind, until he faced a bath full of the toning solution. In an instant, his movements slowed almost to a stop. With great care, using forceps and gloves, he worked for ten minutes before removing the paper.

'Roche!' The scream caused me to stagger against the wall. He strode back into the first room, carrying the print. 'Well? Roche, a better image of the man was never seen.'

There, on a leather-bound blotter, Abraham Lincoln to the very life.

'I can't pay you much to begin with, but you'll not care, will you? Working with Mathew Brady can get you a job anywhere. What was your name?'

AT NIGHT, sitting in an attic room in The Willard, I read through my notes, adding to them occasionally. *Travelling studio must be getting information from both armies. Brady getting word from both sides. How else to find battlegrounds? Too big an area in eastern states to tour at random. Too many photographs of too many battles to be just luck. Sources must be good. Find sources.*

For three days, I scurried about the hotel suite, preparing the gold solution, and becoming conversant with the processes Brady used. The other men ignored my presence, as if I were an intrusive child. Brady himself alternated between overseeing printing and dealing with business matters, but always at high speed.

On the fourth day, one of the many messengers to the suite brought about a response from Brady. The usual frantic action now became manic. Brady and Roche outdid each other in raising their voices, sometimes screaming at each other. The excited activity prevented me from following the page who delivered the man bringing the information. After an hour, Roche made an announcement, again, at the top of his voice. We were to be ready on the morrow to accompany a medical train to the east. The hospital unit was Confederate. Brady himself rarely left The Willard, so Thomas Roche would assume leadership of the group. Tall, thinner than any man I ever saw, with a pronounced Adam's Apple, offset by a massive lump on the left side of his neck, Roche would absent himself from photographs. Like his master, he moved at high speed, though he spoke with a Bowery Boys' drawl. Without saying so, he accepted my inclusion on this trip. He reminded us of his principles: pay no heed to the suffering, but only record it in 'instantaneous views.'

The following day, Roche assembled the other men at the hotel stable to prepare the wagons, leaving me alone to attend Brady. Throughout my career, I have benefitted from chance happenings which other people call Fate. My mother dismissed such talk as *vidskepligt nonsens* – mere superstition. Into the suite, unannounced, came a heavily built Union general, with a loud voice and even louder bearing. Mathew Brady obviously knew the man; indeed, they seemed old friends, from the hand-clasping and back-slapping. The general stated the purpose of his visit: he wished to record his latest uniform with its new insignia in a portrait photograph.

'O'Shaughnessy, prepare a plate, clear the photographic area, and find a whiskey for General Meigs.' Ignoring Brady's inability to remember my name, I did as I was told. Meigs, I had heard of, but had never met.

'Quickly boy, Quartermaster General Meigs is a busy man. Spending all that government money gives the man little time for leisure.' For no apparent reason, Brady tutted to himself, his brow furrowing. I would soon find out why.

'Mathew,' Meigs said, 'give the bellboy a ring, would you? Ask for Billy; he knows my requirements.'

Brady tutted once more, then complied. We set about positioning the general for his portrait against a painted mountain backdrop, in front of which stood the stand which would hold the customer's head still. Despite being over-weight, Meigs carried himself well. His greying hair and beard were carefully trimmed, showing an aggressive jaw line while accentuating sharp blue eyes. By the time we were ready to take the exposure, the bellhop 'Billy' came to the suite.

'Hold on a few minutes, Billy, my lad. I've a little commis-sion for you. The usual, you know.'

When we had captured the man's likeness, Meigs downed his whiskey and called the bellboy to him.

'You know what I'm after, Billy.' He extracted coins from a purse and pressed them into Billy's hand. 'Blonde, with pleasing shape and obliging nature. Be off now, and I'll double that if you're back in half an hour.' Waving his empty glass at me, he spoke to Brady. 'If I might make free with one of your rooms for the afternoon, old friend.'

'We are old friends, Montgomery, and you know I don't hold with this, not on my premises. Consort with whores all you please, but don't ask me to approve or accommodate.'

'You're a pious old Irish Catholic, Mathew Benjamin Brady. It's your single failing. I'll see myself out and make my own arrangements. Let me know when the portrait's ready.'

The knowledge I gained during that hour would later ensure the success of my mission: General Meigs liked the company of blonde girls with a pleasing shape. Like me.

. . .

Since joining the Pinkerton Agency, I have travelled across the country by train, horse and a sweet mule ignobly named Beelzebub. I have never been more miserable than I was in the Brady's Travelling Studio Caravan. Four black wagons, whose enormous wheels jolted at every hole and stretch of scree, clattered along at an uncomfortable pace. I found myself squeezed into a youth-sized gap between barrels of evil-smelling chemicals and camera equipment. After a mile, I was uneasy; after an hour I was bruised from bouncing up and down, side to side; after a day I was questioning my sanity in asking to join this crew.

As I guessed, Mathew Brady played the two sides against each other. While setting up the portrait session, I had overheard General Meigs talking with surprising naivety about his coming movements. Twice, I slipped into Brady's suite at night, searched piles of documents, and discovered letters from George Pickett, an officer of General Longstreet's Division. From what he wrote, t`here was no doubt the Confederate Army was somewhere in the Shenandoah Valley. From what little intelligence Roche and the others let slip, I believed we were now following the Army of Northern Virginia, attempting to catch the rearmost auxiliary units.

After three days of tortured jolting, I spied through a hole in the black canvas men in red, green, and blue uniforms. From what I could see, many of these men were dressed in clothing which was anything but uniform. Conventional kepis and officers' military headgear were often replaced by straw hats or battered, patched Stetsons. Though lieutenants and above still boasted boots, some of the infantry wore cloth bindings, or in some cases had no footwear at all.

I heard Roche in discussion with a captain with the First Artillery Battalion of General Longstreet's Corps. Following a snarling exchange, the captain allowed us through the lines, after first threatening to shoot us as spies.

'The man has forgot General Lee's instruction that we are to be permitted, as impartial correspondents, to accompany the Rebel Army,' Roche announced. 'I convinced him by mentioning that Mister Brady and General Longstreet are old acquaintances from the Mexican War.'

By the time sunset brought its persistent clouds of mosquitos and other flying irritants, our wagons rumbled through a series of campsites before we came upon a major encampment. Here were unmistakable signs of senior commanders: discreet latrines, a musical trio with two superb fiddlers and a banjoist, four tents with unpatched canvas. Roche received permission from a company officer to set up our carts at the far side of a stream.

An hour later, among curious visitors, all eager to inspect our equipment, an officer of striking appearance joined us. Smoking a brown bone pipe which matched his eyes, this man was dressed in a gorgeous uniform which spoke of an expensive tailor from Nashville or New Orleans. His jacket, cut in the style of a cadet, with short waist and half-tailed back, was picked out in glittering gold braid. His scarlet breeches showed similar tailoring. A cavalryman's knee-high boots sparkled in the light of our campfire, as did the plated spurs. Almost all soldiers and officers of the CSA, because of problems with shaving, wore chest-long beards. This officer displayed a trimmed moustache and chin beard, the same colour as the curls which sprang from his red and blue kepi. As I often did when meeting handsome men, I viewed him with the eye of a theatrical producer. Here was a dashing rogue, straight from *Darlinda's Deception*. Approaching our encampment, he whistled a tune, accompanying the nearby band's rendition of an Irish melody.

'Gentlemen. Forgive my intruding on your company. I was just curious to see how these marvels work,' he said. For a moment, my heart raced as he peered at me through the campfire smoke before he spoke.

'Your pardon, gentlemen… and young lady,' he went on, doffing his cavalry cap in my direction.

'George,' a massively built companion said, slapping him on the shoulder, 'your eye for the ladies is mistaken on this occasion. That, or you must acquire one of those fashionable monocles when next in Atlanta. The young lady you speak of is a boy. One of the photographers.'

As I pulled my cap further down over my forehead, Roche crossed to the officer and introduced himself, who then replied.

'George Pickett, Major General, at your service.'

General Pickett. George Pickett, the man whose letters I found at The Willard. And he saw through my disguise, did he? If so…. In this third year of the war, women were being shot as spies by both sides, old notions of chivalry long since abandoned. I froze.

'My apologies, sir, for offence given to your young assistant. Though I swear, by the light of this fire, that young man has all the appearance of a lady, and a beauty at that. Those eyes… quite deceiving in a young fellow.'

'James Kemper, also Major General, of Kemper's Brigade, Virginia Volunteers,' the stout man said. 'Also, at your service. My purblind colleague, vain as an Atlanta belle, was of a mind to request a sitting when it is light.'

'Just so, Mister Roche. We will pay handsomely. My friend Kemper, since the blackest, fullest facial hair of the Confederacy hides his politician's face, will not be persuaded. But I might convince Old Pete to sit as well.'

The band meantime had struck up 'Lorena', the favoured song of both armies. Pickett was soon crooning along, as he wheeled his comrade towards their own area. In my time as an agent – before and after this incident – I was never closer to discovery than at that moment. George Pickett's infallible eye for the ladies was exactly that. Of the dozens, even hundreds, of people deceived by my disguises, General Pickett came closest to unmasking me. It was well after midnight before I persuaded myself that I had not lost my ability with the theatrical disguise. About that time, my heartbeat returned to normal, and the flushing left my face.

Even before the group of officers arrived for their portrait sitting, I made important discoveries. With Generals Longstreet – Old Pete – Kemper and Pickett, this was the headquarters of the Army of Northern Virginia. If I could find out in which direction they were travelling, I might guess where they intended to face McClellan. Often, men in authority disregard servants and ships' stewards as having any importance. Such people are excellent sources of information, especially if they are ill-treated or badly paid. I could now add photographers to this list of those to be ignored by busy men. Roche worked on setting up a booth to capture images of these distinguished officers of the Confederacy; as he did so, the subjects talked freely. Mainly, their conversation was of little consequence, but among this chaff, two names recurred: Sharpsburg and Hagerstown. Just as important, I learned that a force under confederate General Hill had been detached to assault Harper's Ferry. Though no military strategist, I knew this meant Lee's army was divided, reduced in size by at least five thousand men. It was time to find the man who would replace me on Roche's team. And he was three miles behind.

'THEY WILL ACCEPT you as a photographer from London. Your facial scarring, you might say, is the result of an unfortunate reaction with acid. Your accent will give your story credence. If you enter the Confederate camp with your second forged letter from Morse, Roche will ask no questions. He will be too busy to care. Tell him I've headed back for more supplies of gold filings.'

'It might have occurred to you to congratulate me for following your route so well, were you not an ungrateful Swedish strumpet,' Cornet said, rifling his saddlebags before producing the forged letter.

'If Brady's wagons had not left a trail a blind buffalo could follow, my own marking of trees surely would. Be about your business, Mister Bellman, of the London Print and Photography Society. *Gör ditt jobb.*'

'Always the final word, even in Swedish.'

THE FIRST PART of the plan accomplished, I now had to find McClellan's Army of the Potomac, and then convince him to act. No simple task. From what I overheard in Washington, I believed General Meigs, with an advance detachment, might be travelling parallel to the rebel army. The roads here were not worth that name. Lanes overgrown with tangle weed, trappers' trails, a series of streams running west to east: I took these, always heading east in the hope of finding Meigs. Although mosquitos are more common in the southern states, those here in Maryland were plentiful enough to cause me annoyance, especially in this damp, warm weather of September. Late that evening, I smelt wood smoke; following that, a bugle call, muted by the prolific river birch. An army camp.

Union pickets, I discovered, were less vigilant that their rebel counterparts, allowing me to get within a mile of the general's encampment unchallenged. Dismounting, I made ready to enter the camp. In the first year of the war, I used the disguise called 'Dakota Jane' during a period when I posed as a travelling entertainer. Now, with the same fringed buckskin jacket and trousers, cavalry-style hat, turned up at the side, and flowing gold yellow and blue ribbons in my hair, I again became Jane. My troupe of dancers, I would allege, were currently twenty miles back, and would entertain the boys in blue before battle. I believed I might persuade Meigs to take me into his confidence and devise a way to bring McClellan to the field. After all, General Meigs had a liking for blondes with a pleasing shape. Like me.

Still unchallenged, I rode into camp. Shocked at the lack of sentries, I smiled my way towards the middle of the encampment, to the sound of whistles and raucous calling. The first sentry, after questioning me, led me to a captain who was less than welcoming.

'We've had spies, women,' he said. 'Washington's riddled with them. That Willard Hotel… recruiting for Jeff Davis. I heard tell the White House too. Show me your credentials.'

'You can see my credentials, like every other soldier in your camp, captain,' I sang, winking, pouting.

'Look, missy…'

'What's this, Captain Denham? A spy, you think? I'll interrogate her in my tent. If she is, well, we know what happens to spies. But she don't look like it to me.'

'Yes, General.'

I winked at the captain again as I looked over my shoulder.

Dressed today in a working uniform, Meigs still exuded authority for all his heaviness. Hair and beard were carefully trimmed, unusual for soldiers preparing for battle. I removed my hat, shaking my hair in a flirtatious manner. It had its effect. The general smiled, offered me a stool, then sat. Having poured himself a drink from a jug – whisky by the smell – he smacked his knee, while leaning towards me.

'Now, what's your story, missy? Why you here, miles from civilised society?'

'General Meigs, I may look like a saloon girl, or a gambler off a riverboat, but I'm in business. For myself. I intend to finish this war rich. I've a troupe of dancing girls, four musicians, a travelling stage. This is my offer. I bring them to your camp, then they'll follow the troops wherever the commanding general heads. We get paid from your quartermaster's funds, plus whatever we can make from the men: gambling, good company…'

'If I pay for a brothel to accompany the army, imagine what they'll say back in Washington,' he said, still not offering me a drink. 'And after this war, I intend to enter the Senate. Can't afford any scandal.'

'And, of course, a man as distinguished as you can never be associated with whores.'

Had he still been drinking, he would have spluttered. As it was, his breath sharpened. Until now, he had been looking at me as a spy, or more likely, a cheap camp follower. Had I just hinted I knew about his whoring?

'Have we met before?' he asked, eyes narrowing.

I shook my head and stared at the jug. 'If you were to offer me a pull at your whisky, we might do business. No whores, no fleecing the men. Straight business deal. Straight.'

He picked up the jug but made no other move.

'Convince me,' he said, picking up an expensive wine glass, certainly not standard army issue.

'I will sing for you tonight,' I said, turning my head on side, with a half-smile on my lips. 'For you and your officers. I promise you will be impressed, convinced I am an entertainer.'

He poured me a glass of whisky.

It matters little now, Lorena,
  The past is in the eternal past;

Our heads will soon lie low, Lorena,
Life's tide is ebbing out so fast.
There is a Future! O, thank God!
Of life, this is so small a part!
'Tis dust to dust beneath the sod;
But there, up there, 'tis heart to heart.

THOUGH SINGING IS NOT an especial strength on stage, my dramatic rendering of this poignant song was sure to delight my audience. I had begun unaccompanied, but a banjo player of some ability joined me in the second verse. The huge central campfire gave me all the light I needed, like a stage lit by floodlight. First officers, then the rest of the men, formed a deep semi-circle. I wore my White Queen dress and tiara. The dramatic effect would have delighted Hannah. So would the applause. I whispered to the musician, who nodded.

"ALL QUIET ALONG THE POTOMAC TONIGHT!"
Hark! Was it the night wind that rustled the leaves
Was it moonlight so wondrously flashing?
It looks like a rifle -- "Ah! Mary, good-bye!"
And the lifeblood is ebbing and splashing
All quiet along the Potomac tonight
No sound save the rush of the river;
While soft falls the dew on the face of the dead -
The picket's off duty forever
"All quiet along the Potomac tonight!"

THIS SECOND SONG, reminding soldiers of fallen comrades and the bitterness of homesickness, worked its magic. Many had tears in their eyes. The thunderous applause, the atmosphere I had created: there was no disputing that I was an entertainer. Meigs crossed to me.

'Convinced.'

ALTHOUGH HE SPENT most of the day with maps and engineers, the general found time to spend with me, using the excuse of arranging for my troupe to join his men. I am aware of the effect my looks and charm have on men. My father would have ignored it; my mother would have first scolded me, then refused me dinner. As a beauty herself, mother was used to attention, but chose to ignore it. Most of the officers, deprived of female company, vied with Meigs for my company, without success.

It was time well spent. By the end of the second day, I had a clear idea of the intended movements of the army. I guessed the expected major battle would occur somewhere between Hagerstown and Turner's Gap. Still McClellan moved too slowly. Meigs, for all his faults, was a soldier committed to the Union cause. I overheard two angry conversations with officers about the need to get the army towards Antietam Creek. The general sent gallopers daily, urging speed. The president, I heard, sent telegrams daily, urging speed. And still McClellan moved too slowly.

If I were to make a success of my mission, I had to act. Hearing that a detachment of the Twenty-Seventh Indiana Volunteers was en route to Hagerstown, I persuaded Meigs I to let me join them, on the pretext of scouting suitable camp-sites for entertaining the men. The detail headed north by west, scouting signs of enemy movement. Once again, the familiar lanes, trails, streams, and mosquitos. The next day, we came upon what had been a military camp, recently abandoned.

'Johnny Reb, for sure,' a sergeant leading the detail

muttered. He scraped the dirt where horse lines had been, sniffed the dung, and spat. 'Yesterday, maybe even this mornin'.'

'What's your name, sergeant?' I asked.

'John Bloss, ma'am. This here's Corporal Mitchell. If you lookin' fer a place to set up, I reckon this is mebbe a bit close fer comfort. Your gals might be put off'n their dancin' by the sound of our guns, blastin' them boys in grey back to Kentucky. The rest o' you men, there, search this camp. See if they left any makins fer supper. Sloosh, the rebs likes, and mighty fine it goes with coffee salted with sour mash.'

As the sergeant described the taste of bacon fat and grain, one of his troopers called to Corporal Mitchell.

'See here, Sarge,' Mitchell said, holding a package. 'Them careless bastards has left their cigars. Don't clean up after themselves. Know you're partial to them Virginia cigars. Here.'

Mitchell saw only the contents, or perhaps he could not read. After catching the bundle, Bloss realised what he held in his hand.

'Lord God Almighty, look at this. Mitch, look here. Good God Almighty! It's the rebel battle plan. Jesus! They've wrapped their orders round three Virginia cigars.'

When Mitchell shook his head, Bloss turned to me.

'Kin you read, ma'am? I'm right, I'm sure of it. Kin you read?'

Though at first disbelieving, when I understood what I held in my hand, and its importance, my hand shook. I read it twice, then again. I read it aloud:

Special Orders, No. 191

Hdqrs. Army of Northern Virginia

September 9, 1862

The citizens of Fredericktown being unwilling while overrun by members of this army, to open their stores, to give them confidence, and to secure for officers and men purchasing supplies for benefit of this command, all officers and men of this army are strictly prohibited from visiting Fredericktown except on business, in which cases they will bear evidence of this in writing from division commanders. The Provost-Marshal in Fredericktown will see that his guard rigidly enforces this order.

Major Taylor will proceed to Leesburg, Virginia, and arrange for transportation of...

And it went on. About five hundred words, ten paragraphs. And at the bottom:

By command of General R. E. Lee

R.H. Chilton, Assistant Adjutant General

Special Order no 191

The entire detachment gathered round, though none understood the importance of what I read, apart from Bloss. Rubbing my forehead and eyes to focus, I made my decision.

'Sergeant, take charge of this paper for a few minutes. When I am ready, you will accompany me back to General Meigs' headquarters.'

The man's mouth fell open.

'Ma'am, Miss Dakota...'

'Sergeant Bloss, I am Major Astrid Karlsson, ranking woman in the US Army, Special Agent in the Secret Service. Set up a blanket tent there. When I have changed, strike the tent, make ready to follow me at the gallop. Before we leave, hear this: your discovery today may bring about an end to this war. If General McClellan moves quickly.'

In ten minutes, I emerged from the makeshift tent, dressed in full blue uniform, with a Navy Colt pistol at my waist and sabre hanging from my belt. I had no time to humour the men or enjoy their shock at my transformation. Ordering them to store my long canvas carrying bag, I pocketed the paper and set off.

As well as the roads allowed us, we galloped the twenty

miles between Frederick and the railroad tracks, beyond which Meigs had made camp.

Meigs was once again in conference with his engineers when my arrival was announced.

'Major who… what is this nonsense? Who did you say?'

Minutes mattered. I had no time to discuss my identity with the general.

'Major Karlsson, at your service, General Meigs.'

The others in the tent stepped back, as Meigs leaned across his travelling chest, glaring at me.

'I should believe that Dakota Jane, the entertainer, is now a spy? For us? Major Karlsson, I have heard of. President Lincoln gave her rank. Why should I trust you now? Since you deceived me once already.'

'Twice, sir. But if you read this letter from my principal, you will see that I am who I say I am. Quickly, General Meigs. There is no time.'

His face whitened as he read my note.

'Sir,' I said. 'Now read this. Take a moment to appreciate its importance, then send me to General McClellan. He must move now.'

Having handed him Special Order No. 19, I waited for a reaction.

'This is… it's right. I know Chilton, the officer who wrote this paper. We exchanged cards once before a duel. He and I were friends, till he… I know his writing. Lee's battle plans, by God! Holy God! This means Hill is still at Harper's Ferry. We outnumber Lee three to one, maybe more. Even McClellan must see the need for a fight. If we strike now, we can end this. Major Karlsson, Dakota Jane, whoever you are right now, take a fresh horse, the best we have. Get to McClellan. I'll move this force to Frederick.'

As I saluted, he called me back.

'Twice, Major? You said you…'

'At The Willard Hotel, sir. One of Mathew Brady's assistants.'

'You knew about… when you spoke about… the women. You knew.' His eyes flickered with an expression I could not read. 'I'm glad you're on our side, Major Karlsson. A dangerous lady.'

'And the duel, sir. You and Chilton?'

'I came down with pox,' he answered. 'No, not that kind, chickenpox. You are a *very* dangerous lady.'

McClellan kept me waiting. I expected no better, since we were enemies. Gripping the scabbard of my sabre, tightening the fingers till they hurt, I recalled our previous meetings. The first occasion was when the president announced my promotion to the post of Major. Of all the senior military staff present, only McClellan voiced disapproval. The words he used to describe me I will never forget. The second time, when McClellan offered excuse after excuse for delaying, I humiliated him by producing evidence about the relative size of the armies.

We hated each other. Yet I could not believe, with the chance to end the war and win glory, McClellan would fail to act. Even allowing for his wish to spite me, the man's rewards for winning would be huge. He was rumoured to have ambitions to occupy the White House; it was well known that he despised President Lincoln, calling him 'that grotesque gorilla.' My fingers throbbed as I muttered to myself in Swedish: *Gör den plikt, Allamänt McClellan.*

The longer I waited, the more I looked at my watch, the more I could envisage a battle lost instead of the decisive victory. An hour after my arrival – an hour – I was shown into his presence by an officer wearing the gold aiguillettes of a general's aide. This man, at least, showed respect for my rank.

'Major Karlsson, sir,' he announced.

McClellan, a cigar hanging loose from the side of his mouth, continued to inspect Special Order No. 19, which I had sent to him on my arrival.

'I have no doubt, Brevet Major, that this lady is about to give me advice. Watch and see how long it takes for her to do so.' The aide at my side shuffled. 'I have little time for you today, madam. There are matters to which I must attend. This piece of wrapping paper – cigars, I am told – is supposed to be plans for Lee's movement of troops. And I am to take this seriously? Do I believe that the Army of Northern Virginia, all seventy thousand of them, are commanded by idiots who cannot keep their orders safe in their pants?'

He rose, eyes blazing, voice now close to a hysterical scream. He knocked over the stool he ought to have offered me.

'Most of all, I am to move my army on the word of a Swedish actress?'

Though I resented doing so, I opened with words I did not mean.

'With respect, sir, the matter you must attend to is to set upon Lee's army this day. Before he can call up General Hill's corps from Harper's Ferry. Even with that force, the rebel army numbers less that forty thousand men. The opportunity to bring this war to a close lies with you, sir. The document you hold is genuine, Chilton's handwriting recognised by General Meigs.'

'Meigs, a man who ruts his way across Washington! And you. You presume to tell me the size of Lee's forces. You, a foreign agent who whored her way into Lincoln's favour. Get her from my sight!'

'General, is it correct that you intend to ignore the evidence before you, and once again delay moving the Army of the Potomac against the enemy?' I said, my temper rising by the second.

'Remove her from my tent!' he screamed.

'General George Brinton McClellan, you are little more than a coward, afraid to take the field against an army half the size of your own. Nor indeed is it your army, but that of the United States of America, whose commander in Abraham Lincoln. You are a disgrace to the uniform you wear, and a traitor to the Union cause.'

For the first and only time in my career, I lost my temper with a man because he belittled me. Because of the importance of seizing the moment, I made a serious tactical error. McClellan squared his shoulders, looked me in the eye, and addressed his aide.

'Brevet Major, arrest her. She will remain confined until I convene a court martial. The penalty for insubordination to a superior officer in the field is death by firing squad.'

'Sir,' the man at my side said, 'I am not sure I can arrest her. She is of higher rank than me. General, I ask you to reconsider this action…'

'Brevet Major Custer, I command this army. If you wish to retain your temporary rank, do as I have commanded you. Else you will find yourself charged with refusing to obey an order.'

On 16th September 1862, I was placed under arrest by George Custer. A man who would feature in my life many years later, in the Black Hills, Dakota, at a river called Little Bighorn.

THROUGHOUT MY CAREER I have spent more uncomfortable nights than the one in the temporary prison of McClellan's command: like the jail in Tallahassee, or the stable in Hampton. In none, however, have I been as fearful for the future of the Union cause.

Two days later, I discovered my fears were justified. Just after dawn on the 18th, I was marched to McClellan's headquarters. Black clouds had formed overnight. At the very moment I followed the guard, the storm exploded, sheets of icy rain sweeping over the encampment. The same aide, Brevet Major Custer, met me. As history would record, George Custer was impetuous and given to bursts of emotion. That day, with eyes downcast and lips forming the straightest of lines, he saluted, a courtesy to which an arrested officer is not entitled. He strode across the duckboards to McClellan's tent, back as straight as a musket's ramrod, like one of the wooden puppets in McCafferty's Magical Toys act.

'General McClellan, Major Karlsson.'

For fully two minutes, I remained at attention as McClellan shuffled the papers on his travelling desk. Contrary to protocol, Custer repeated the introduction. There was a note, not of impatience, but of anger in his reminder, risking a reprimand from his commander. McClellan fired a fierce glance at his aide, who, unflinching, returned it in full measure.

'Remain at attention, madam. You too, Custer.' He refused to look up from his papers.

I had spent a night in a converted supply wagon, I was filthy, and I recognised the sense of calamity about the camp.

'General McClellan, with respect,' I said, 'you cannot have it two ways. If, as your addressing me as 'madam' suggests, you regard me as a civilian, you have no right to give me orders. On the other hand, if you recognise my rank – a commission conferred by our commander-in-chief – you should address me as 'colonel'. In either case, I request an account of what has taken place. In the short journey from my prison to here, I saw areas of this camp shielded from sight by massive tents, such as might be used for hospitals. There has been a battle.'

McClellan gripped the roll of papers he was holding till his knuckles turned red, then white. With his jaw clenched, the chin beard protruded from his face, like a ham actor in a melodrama. If this were the final act of *The Villain of Vienna*, he would blow his own brains out.

'It has been suggested that I release you from the charge you were facing. The suggestion comes from Washington. I don't know how the news of your arrest was conveyed to the War Office, but if I find that any of my officers have been in contact with Stanton, they will face charges themselves. Dismissed.'

'There has been a battle, sir?' I persisted.

'There has been a battle at Antietam Creek. A great victory for the Union army, under my command. Custer, show this officer out.'

Again, like a parody of a soldier in a theatrical farce, Custer saluted, clicked his heels, turned, and escorted me from the tent. His every movement bordered on insubordination. A few steps from the headquarters, Custer removed his cape and draped it over my shoulders.

'Your pardon, Major, but before you leave for Washington, there are… you must see for yourself the nature of this great victory for the Union army.'

He led me over the rise above McClellan's headquarters to a vast tented expanse of what had been fields. Row after row after row of tents. An area, fast becoming a quagmire in the torrential rain, not quite deadening the appalling sounds.

'Pick any of the tents. They are all the same: hospital tents holding the dead and dying of the Battle of Antietam.'

Since Bull Run, I had witnessed the aftermath of battle. Always the same. Tents of howling, vomiting, crying men. Calling for their mother, calling for God, calling for death. The first hospital tent I entered was as before: soldiers lying on sacks, or on their capes, or on the sodden ground, since the number of beds was exceeded by the number of casualties. At the far end, a surgeon sawing through the leg from a screaming victim. He used a crude carpenter's saw. The teeth gnarled the flesh it chewed into, before reaching the bone, accompanied by that terrible grinding noise. The doctor, the assistant holding the man down, the soldier himself: all knew the pointlessness of the torture. If shock did not kill him, gangrene would. Just outside the tent, barrels full of amputated human parts: legs, arms, hands, fingers, feet. Beyond that, an adjoining tent containing the mangled corpses of those already released from their torture. The smells were always the same: the sweetness of blood, the bitter acrid stench of vomit, the foulness of excrement.

Stepping into the storm was a relief. Custer led me well beyond the charnel house, half a mile from headquarters. Even then, there were more avenues of tents. Finding a place where someone had draped a scrap of canvas across a snake rail fence, the man squatted down and pointed to a dry spot where I might sit.

'Did you contact the War Office about me?' I asked.

'That would be a court martial offence. I've already faced one of those. In the light of all this, does it matter a barrel of salt pork?'

When he offered me a flask to drink from, for once I did. The unpleasantly sweet spirit – some unnamed southern whisky – at least took away the imagined taste of sickness in my mouth.

'I'm a soldier, Major; so are you. We've seen battles, and we've seen mistakes by commanders. But here. Him. What if you have an army of ten men? You are facing only two. But over there, your enemy has another eight, coming to join them. They shout: Wait on. We know you could finish us off, but wait till the others join us, and it'll be a fair fight. So, what do you do?'

'And that's what happened?'

'After you brought the Reb plan of attack, we could have finished this war that day.'

Custer took the flask, drained it, then threw it with all his strength into the storm.

'The battle? How did…'

'Our commander waited and waited and waited. Till Hill's corps arrived from Harper's Ferry and made it a fair fight. There will never be another day like it.'

'How many men did we lose?' I asked. Even as I did so, in my mind I could see wave after wave of men in grey, killing wave after wave of men in blue. Bayonets, howitzers, bullets, cannon, mortars, rockets. Men blown to pieces, with nothing left to identify them; men with bellies ripped open by sabre cuts, men without heads, arms, legs; men drowning in puddles and in their own blood; men trampled by horses and by other men.

'I can't count. Don't suppose we'll ever know. Five thousand, ten thousand.'

I almost said it couldn't be that many, but I stopped. I had seen the tents.

'When you get back to Washington, Major Karlsson, you've got to tell them. Till we find a general that knows this business, our war will never end. It'll just go on and on.'

Standing, he dug a hole in the mud with his right boot, drew a cigar from his tunic, crushed it, then threw it in the hole. As if in doing so, he had crushed Virginia. Like his general should have.

· · ·

I WAS SADDLING MY HORSE, preparing for the long, dismal return to Washington, when I heard shouting, angry voices following the sound of trundling wagons. And in the cacophony, a voice I recognised. An English accent, with a limitless supply of colourful swearing words.

'It is my understanding that the president has authorised us to record details of any engagement by means of the photography.' Roche's voice accompanying Cornet Livermore's cursing.

'That is no way to speak to officers in the Union army, Cornet Livermore. I'm ashamed of you,' I said, approaching my friend, now seated on one of Brady's wagons. As I did so, Roche, already dismounted, looked at me with eyes wide and mouth open.

'Mister Roche, there is no time for explanations. You knew me as the young assistant with ideas for improving the printing process. I am Major Karlsson, agent of the United States Secret Service. It is understandable that these officers object to recording the death and misery they have just endured. To them, I can only say this: when the people in Michigan, Rhode Island, California, and Florida see these records, they will realise why this carnage must be stopped.'

MY PRINCIPAL GAVE me the choice of being present when General McClellan attended a meeting at the War Office. I accepted, not for reasons of revenge. I would not allow the man to find excuses that might dissuade the president from his decision.

Elegant and well-groomed as always, George McClellan entered Secretary Stanton's Office, ignored me, and sat at the head of the table. No secretaries or military aides were present, meaning an unpleasant silence between the general and me was broken only by McClennan lighting his cigar.

When Stanton entered, he stood at the other man's shoulder, staring straight ahead. McClennan sat for longer than was polite before vacating the chair.

'Why is this person…' the general began, waving his hand in my direction. With cigar still clenched in his teeth, he refused to look at me.

'If you are about to question the presence of Major Karlsson at this meeting, remember you have been summoned to my office to give your own account of the battle which took place at Antietam, near Sharpsburg, Maryland, on the seventeenth of this month. Major Karlsson is a key witness to these events.'

'Major Karlsson was absent from the engagement of which you speak,' McClellan spat, crushing his cigar into a silver ashtray.

'Major Karlsson was absent from that field on your instructions, which action will itself be part of an inquiry.'

I had met Stanton twice before, each time in the presence of the president. Having the appearance of a preacher, with a long, greying beard, soft blue eyes, and black suit, he was nonetheless a feared adversary and fierce defender of President Lincoln. Those eyes now lost their usual melancholy aspect, firing warnings which McClellan chose to ignore. For some moments, a tense silence replaced the anger already expressed by each man. Lighting a cigar himself, Edwin Stanton invited the general to give his account of the events leading up to the battle, as well as its aftermath.

'You do not wish to hear of the engagement, sir?' McClellan asked.

'The events leading to the battle, and its aftermath only. I have here all the information I require about the battle.' In a movement capable of stopping a drama on stage, Stanton produced a piece of paper, no bigger that the palm of his hand.

For the next hour, General McClellan gave details of the organization of the Army of the Potomac, his intelligence regarding the size of Lee's army, and his preparations 'to sweep the enemy from Maryland.'

'And have you succeeded in this?' Stanton asked, tipping the ash from his cigar into an ashtray. 'Is the Army of Northern Virginia swept from Maryland? Is my information that they still hold territory to the south of the Potomac wrong?'

'Had I not been summoned to this meaningless charade, Lee would even now be on his way back to Richmond.'

'Is it not the case, sir, that Major Karlsson presented you with intelligence about the strength of the enemy and their position two days before the battle? Intelligence that General Hill's Corps was then engaged at Harper's Ferry? Did this intelligence not demand immediate action? Would immediate action not have resulted in the Union army, then almost ninety thousand strong, confronting Lee's twenty thousand men?'

Until that point in meeting, McClellan still had not looked me in the eye.

'Was I to commit my army on the word of a foreign actress? I won a victory! The enemy quit the field.'

'After which you failed to pursue him, once again losing the chance to finish this war.'

Stanton laid down the stub of his cigar and inhaled deeply.

'In 279, King Pyrrhus of Epirus defeated the Roman army at Asculum,' Stanton said. 'His victory cost him the war, his army having suffered so many casualties. Another victory like the one you claim to have won at Antietam will cost the Union this war.'

In a further dramatic movement, Stanton opened the scrap of paper he held, and read.

'Lost to the Army of the Potomac at the battle of Antietam, over twelve thousand casualties. Lost to the Army of Northern Virginia, over ten thousand casualties.'

'As a portion of those engaged, our losses were less than theirs,' McClellan answered. 'And if the purpose of war is to kill the enemy's soldiers, who should care about Confederate losses?'

'I should,' a voice from behind the general said, in the quiet tone of a man saddened by such numbers. 'They are our fellow Americans, George. Someday this war will end. When it does, the Seventeenth of September will be recorded as the blackest day in our history. Twenty-five thousand of our countrymen lost in a day. If this is victory, what must defeat be like?'

President Lincoln's tall body was bent, his shoulders sagging, as if a heavy weight forced him down.

'Secretary Stanton has other figures I wish him to read.'

'You have had forty-three meetings with President Lincoln, at which he urged you to take action. You have received one hundred and seventeen telegrams from President Lincoln urging you to take action. In each case, you have found excuses for not doing so. The army was not ready, there were not sufficient supplies, the weather was against you, the terrain was unsuitable. Most frequently, the enemy's forces were too strong without your receiving reinforcements.'

McClellan stood up, pushing his chair back, and made for the door.

'George, we have not concluded this meeting,' the president said, his voice though soft, still compelling.

'General George Brinton McClellan, by order of the president, you are relieved of command of the Army of the Potomac. You will report to Trenton, New Jersey, for further orders.' Stanton, now standing, made this proclamation as though he were addressing an audience.

'Who will take command of my army?' McClellan asked.

'General Ambrose Burnside will take command of the Army of the Potomac,' Stanton continued.

'The Army of the Potomac. My Army. The army of the people of this United States,' Lincoln went on.

Secretary Stanton followed General McClellan from the room, leaving me alone with the president.

'You have my thanks, and not for the first time, Astrid,' Lincoln said. 'What you achieved in this mission, it should have ended this civil war. But still it goes on. I asked Allan Pinkerton to give you this assignment; you know that. But today is still a momentous one, Major Karlsson. For three reasons. First, after Antietam, the governments of France and Great Britain have contacted Jeff Davis and me. They have withdrawn any support they might have offered the Confederacy. Second, I will today issue The Emancipation Proclamation, freeing over three million slaves. Three million of our citizens, free. Consider that, Major. Third, of course, I have replaced George McClellan with Ambrose Burnside. I'm not sure he's the man to out-think Lee. But I'll find the right one. I'd consider Grant, but they say he drinks.'

I looked at the two cigars in the ashtray and thought of the one Custer had crushed into the mud at Antietam. Three cigars. Like the three found at Frederick. Three cigars, one each for replacing McClellan, for ending the support of foreign governments to the South, for freeing three million Americans.

OF ALL THE photographs in Mathew Brady's exhibition 'The Dead of Antietam', there is one which adds to my already sufficient store of nightmare images. Three men, of which army it is impossible to know, lying dead before a fence. Three sons, fathers, husbands, or lovers. Their faces are so mangled, few features are evident. One man has his arm raised as though he is swimming, one lies with his head under the fence. The third, in the foreground, with only his gaping mouth visible, rests on a battle flag, again unidentifiable. Brady's ninety-five photographs shocked a nation. Line after line after line of corpses, mud, dismembered horses, with appalled soldiers viewing the carnage. Justification enough for desecrating the final moments of thousands of brave men who died at Antietam.

The Battle of Antietam. Three cigars. Ninety-five photographs.

TWO PYTHONS AND A BIG YELLOW BOOL

Like the Black Spot in *Treasure Island*, announcing impending death, the summons lay before me. An appointment with the Director of Social Work Department would not result in my execution but might end in dismissal. Incompetence in relation to a case of child neglect as reported by Strathclyde Police, the letter said. When I consider the events of those few days just before Christmas – an absurd encounter with snakes and entanglement with international criminal gang – I realised the whole business began with a memo.

To: T. Pendleton
From: C. Snoddie
Re: Today's assignment
How are you with reptiles?

THAT MY BOSS had emailed me, with his desk only ten metres away, was not the surprise. Campbell Snoddie was the biggest sloth in Social Work Department. Even expending the effort to articulate a message would have caused his pores to open and excrete some of last evening's house red. The subject of his memo was, however, puzzling. I batted back my reply.

To: C. Snoddie
  From: T. Pendleton
  Re: Your message
  ???

His return memo ordered me to deal with an enquiry at the front desk, after I had seen The Boss, Ms Bann. What at first seemed bizarre now became scary. Lisbeth Bann, Senior Social Worker. This lady dealt with only the most serious matters. Senior Social Workers have extensive powers, with the authority to launch court cases and recommend the removal of a child from the parental home.

'Tammy,' she said, waving a hand at an adjacent chair, 'after you've handled this first nonsense, I want you to look into another matter. Probably a case, possibly serious. Since you're going to the East Docks area, this other thing is only half a mile away. You can investigate both and be done by evening. I might have to involve myself at some point, but you find out what's doing for me, eh? This is a tricky business.'

She handed me a thin folder with the name Janis Beverley on the cover. Although I did not recognise the logo of the referring council, I found on inspection that the two black lions supporting a shield represented Northampton Council. Before I could read the file, Lisbeth explained.

'There's several things here. According to Brooke Wealdon Academy, in Corby, this girl Janis Beverly has disappeared. Although they recorded her as a first-year pupil three years ago, she has not been seen this year. Or much before that, either. We both know 'problem families' will sometimes up sticks and flit when they feel the breath of police or debt collectors on their necks. Sometimes it's drugs, sometimes something worse. According to the Northants Police, the family might be in our area. At this address.' She handed me a slip of paper.

'Here's the second thing. Preliminary enquiries by your friend Laura at Community Police confirm that there is a family living there... but no-one quite knows who. There might be a girl, or not. There might be a thirty-odd year old man, or not. There might be an older man, or not.' My Senior stopped, cracked her knuckles, then went into her false-grin mode.

'So, you want me to go to...' I paused before reading the address, '... 168 Summerlea Drive, East Docks, and investigate? After this other enquiry?'

'Yes, just down the road from the reptile business.' She looked at her cracked knuckles. 'Careful, Tammy. I don't like the smell of this Beverley girl thing. Take someone with you. Someone good.'

'Alfred Santini?' I blurted, without thinking.

She replaced her Ray-Ban glasses, peered over them, and sighed. Saying nothing further, she swivelled her chair and turned her attention to her iMac.

'If you can read over my shoulder, you'll note that an anonymous neighbour reports a child was left unattended over the weekend. The e-mail, sent from an internet café, and therefore untraceable, says we should go there before the Christmas holidays, to prevent abandonment through the holiday period. That means today. I can smell trouble,

Tammy. Take someone. And maybe a police presence. But first, see the postie.'

THE SOCIAL WORK DEPARTMENT office in Dalbeattie Street is a warren of tiny offices behind brown oak doors, connected by green and white tiled corridors and possessing a Victorian smell. I often imagined difficult officials or troublesome parents being led around for several minutes, deposited in a cell, then forgotten about. I would soon wish this to be the case with the postie I found at the reception desk.

The earnest, heavily built postman, blue sleeves rolled to the elbow, stood almost at attention as I arrived.

'Yous will have to do something; it's no' right, that. I wisny gonny let it pass. Yous will have to do something.'

Sensing an irksome case, so near Christmas, I led the man left, right, right again and downstairs, hoping perhaps to lose him. Tenacious as the terriers he fended off daily, he was still there when I unlocked the door. You get used to the unusual at the SWD, but this one floored me. There was a lot of puffing, and moralistic exclamations, and brow-mopping, but the crux of his story was this. Delivering a long, thin cardboard package to a flat at 10C Station Rise, and believing it was fresh flowers, the intrepid postman rang the bell, handed over the box, and prepared to leave. The recipient, a sluttish twenty-something, ignored several crawling infants and a pug, then forbade the man to go until she checked 'if they were all right.' Approaching him with a Stanley knife, the woman opened one end of the carton and tipped out the contents.

'Snakes. Two bloody great python things just slid out of the box and right into the kitchen, followed by the weans and the dug. Jesus Christ, I've delivered all sorts, but never bloody giant snakes. If yous go up there, you'll find nae weans, only snakes wi' big babies' lumps in their bellies, an' a wumman howlin' about her lost dug.'

Moments later, standing in front of Campbell Snoddie, I remonstrated with him.

'What am I supposed to do? Eh? Do you think I'm Indiana Jones? Does it say on my contract: must tame ferocious wild animals in the course of duties? I won't go up there, Campbell.'

'Tammy,' he said, forced to open his mouth at last, 'we must investigate. Children may be at risk. And Indiana Jones wouldn't have helped; he's afraid of snakes.'

'No bloody wonder he's afraid of snakes,' I screamed, much to the amusement of my colleagues, who were not going reptile hunting. 'So am I.'

'So, take Daft Alfred with you,' Cameron said, grinning as he bit the top of his chocolate snowman. 'Send him in first; he'll love it.'

Alfred, the newest recruit to Social Work, was callow, childish and often the butt of jokes. Despite this, I liked the boy's honesty and lack of cynicism. Besides, he would face up to the pythons, trying to be an intrepid hero in front of me.

As WE NEARED the reptile house, I lost my nerve. I phoned my contact at Community Police and asked her to meet us at the snake-infested Flat 10C, Station Rise. Alfred, too young to be cautious, was for rushing in, unaided. I told him to park his bottom on the edge of the raised flower bed and wait. Despite his naiveté, I liked the boy enough not to want to see an Alfred-shaped lump rippling along a huge reptile's belly.

As I explained standard procedure where child endanger-ment in relation to wild animals – a procedure I made up on the spot – my friend WPC Watson arrived. I led them both up the stairs – the lift naturally being out of order – to the fateful door. I listened, ear hard against the red paintwork, but heard neither wailing nor slithering. Laura rapped, announcing the presence of the police. After a minute's indoor yelling, the door opened to reveal the lady the postie had described. He was not wrong in his appraisal.

Black hair tousled in the manner of Bellatrix Lestrange, the woman wore what might have been a negligee, or perhaps a sloppy jumper. In either case, her boobs were barely concealed. Not, I felt, to increase her allure, more because she hadn't sewed missing buttons back on. Alfred, nevertheless, ogled with childish vigour.

When the constable explained our presence, the woman disappeared into the main room, returning with a pair of five-inch-long grass snakes, one wriggling in each hand. While 'Mam' cursed the postie, police, and nosey social work bastards, the infantile inhabitants crawled into view, neither wearing nappies, nor being too careful about what they stuffed into their mouths. Fortunately, the pug cleaned both their faces and their behinds, although, unfortunately, not in that order. Before we left, I informed the lady that, though the children were in no immediate danger, I had seen enough to raise a case file for child neglect. After being told once more that I was a nosey social work bitch, I grabbed the still leering Alfred and escaped with the policewoman, pausing only to smack Alfred for his immature lechery.

I had got used to Daft Alfred, so I took him to our next port of call. At least he was fit and keen. The more I thought about this, the more I felt my Christmas hamper might have to wait till twelfth night. Lisbeth Bann was many things, but, having an outstanding nose for trouble, she was rarely wrong.

'Like the Wild West here, the East Docks, isn't it?' Alfred asked, glancing at the de-wheeled Tesco trolley. There were also drug dealers' choices of transport – Mercedes and

Suzuki Swifts – half-mounted on the rubble that once were pavements.

'Beirut, more like,' I muttered. 'Find 163.'

The four-in-a-block houses stopped at 161, then continued at 171, after the Golden Gate Kebab. I parked our car at 181, a safe distance from our destination. As we walked to where 163 should be, what we saw was a split-level 'fort', of the kind made popular in 60's new towns, set off the road. Out of place here, though. There seemed at least three entrances: one each front and back, and one to what might have been a garage. Todda, the kebab shop owner, though pleasant and chatty, could tell us nothing about 163 or its inhabitants.

'That girl is waving at us,' Alfred said, pointing to a child of indeterminate age sitting astride an old BMX. I took this as an invitation, and crossed to where she sat, elbows on high handlebars. With wild brown hair straggling down her back, except for one tail caught in a blue ribbon to the right of her head, she had sharp eyes. She wore what might have been a grey school uniform and had a satchel strung across the left shoulder.

'Are you the police?' she asked, in a voice which surprised me. The standard question should have been: *Yoos the Polis?* After either a positive or negative reply, she would have told us to f*** off. This was an articulate child. Something else out of place. The anonymous tip (unheard of in the East Dock area), the strange, isolated house, and now this polite girl. My senior's nose for major issues seemed infallible.

Showing her my identification, I asked about the owners of 163. The Kennedys lived there, she told us. Yes, there was a girl, about her own age, though they never spoke. There were two men, a father, and a grandfather. She thought the teenager was called Jean or something, and that she went to a posh school in Kilmacolm.

'We're looking for a missing child,' Alfred blurted. Tutting, I told myself to explain to him later that we never revealed more than was necessary. BMX girl wheeled away, seemed to have second thoughts, then biked back.

'I've heard crying from that garage thing at night,' she said, before taking off for good this time.

When I got no reply from any of the three doors, I texted my senior, then contacted the police, when Alfred interrupted.

'No one in,' he said, trying to sound like a mage.

'In this part of the town, a no-reply usually means they're figuring out if we're the law or the loan sharks,' I answered. But no reply from WPC Laura Watson meant she was busy on a job. 'Let's head back to the office.'

By the time we got there, Lisbeth was typing up an SWD Form 16A (Suspected Child at Risk. Immediate Action). She herself had contacted the police, asking that Constable Wilson attend our offices, prior to a Search of Premises order.

It was already dark when we returned to East Docks, with a chill winter drizzle limiting visibility. As we passed Station Rise, I waved to our python friends. Despite being an area of great deprivation, most of the flats had Christmas trees up; some even had garish outside lights. Nothing at our target house, though.

Laura approached what seemed to be the main entrance and knocked. Nothing. When she tried the garage door, her knock produced a heavy, metallic echo. Finally, at the rear, a light showed. A caricature of a man opened the door. With spine bent over, snow white hair, and corresponding beard, he was the image of Grandpaw Broon from *The Sunday Post*. All it needed was a pipe and flat cap for us to believe Oor Wullie lived next door. He led us into a sitting room, sparsely furnished with only a cheap self-assembly three-piece suite, four chairs, and a table. The walls, from the smell, had been recently painted off-white, while the flooring was thin, faux parquet lino. Alfred and I sat on the settee while Laura began her questions.

'My son lives here, just for now. Aye, his wee girl Esther, too,' he answered. They were both out shopping at Aldi, he explained. He himself didn't live here.

'We were told her name was Jean,' I said.

'Aye, that's right,' he said, scrambling for answers. 'Esther Jean.'

'Have you heard of a girl called Janis Beverley?' A shake of his head. A little too quick, I thought. After explaining more fully why we were here, Laura asked to see the rest of the house. When those two went upstairs, I told Alfred to use our digital camera to take photos of the place.

'This whole thing stinks,' I whispered. 'Nobody really lives here.' When Alfred shrugged his shoulders, I explained. 'No telly, no VCR, no photos. I'll bet there's no food in the kitchen. Go and see.' I was right.

Laura and the man identifying himself as Jock Kennedy came back down. My friend opened her notebook.

'I must inform you, Mister Kennedy, I am not satisfied with anything I've seen. The young girl we're looking for has neither bed nor possessions in this house. This lady here, the social worker, has a permit which allows us to search these premises more fully.'

Grandpaw Broon collapsed into a chair.

'Right, right,' he said, hand over his eyes. 'He keeps her in the garage. That's a' I know. It's my son, he's a psycho. Mental. Ye'll no' get in there, for he's got the place bolted up. I came today to get her oot.'

He was right about the garage: we could not get in. The door into the garage from the house, as well as the outside door, seemed to be reinforced from inside. Within the hour,

Laura's Inspector Collins and a sergeant arrived, since we were now dealing with imprisonment, at the very least. Still unable to force our way in, the inspector sent for the Fire Service, who had the equipment to allow access.

As a fan of *London's Burning*, I was not surprised that the firefighters were highly skilled in solving problems like this. Using acetylene torches and bolt-cutters, they forced entry through the interior door. The crowd inside the house was growing. Despite her earlier wish to stay at arm's length, Lisbeth Bann turned up, instructing Alfred to photograph everything in the garage, since she now believed we might have to account for our actions in court. Inspector Collins, as senior officer present, entered first, stamped down two steps, as though to frighten ghosts, before finding a light switch. Though years as a social worker have made a cynic of me, the thought of what we might find here was terrifying. I clutched Alfred's arm. A horrible pause.

'Nothing. Not a damn thing,' Collins shouted, his voice echoing round the stone garage.

Having had visions of a decaying corpse, or chains, or evidence of abuse, I laughed out loud in relief.

'Just junk,' Laura said. 'Old furniture, toys, rubbish.'

The entrance to the street was so reinforced by steel bars that even the intrepid firefighters would have struggled to get through. Again, Lisbeth instructed Alfred to record everything.

'That's quite a nice chair, that there,' I commented, sitting on the furniture in question. 'I've seen these in *Bargain Hunt*. Antique, worth maybe fifty pounds.'

Jock Kennedy, moving quickly for an elderly man, picked up a tarpaulin from the corner, threw it over the chair and me, then explained.

'My wife's old armchair,' he said. 'There's a wobbly leg, so you'd better get aff it.'

Alfred, after photographing all the rest of the junk, began playing with a solitaire board, one of these circular wooden affairs where you scoot a marble round and try to do something with the other 'bools.' The old man laughed as he picked up the marble in the centre, much larger than the others, and a vibrant yellow colour. He rolled it in the palm of his hand before pocketing it. Laura, watching this, shrugged her shoulders, since there was no objection to picking up a kid's toy.

'Maybe we could wrap up some of this stuff with these old newspapers, for evidence?' Alfred asked.

'Evidence of what?' the inspector barked. 'Bloody waste of time. Ms Bann, next time your team has a hunch that a child is missing, tell them to get some fucking facts before making a song and dance about nothing. Bloody Christmas Eve.' His parting festive remarks. When we left 163, we discovered that Grandpaw Broon had taken off.

By now it was midnight. Christmas Eve. And I could picture myself typing up report after report on this shambles of an investigation. As we drove back to the office, my head buzzed with unanswered questions. Where was the father? Was Jock Kennedy the grandfather? Why had someone gone to such lengths to barricade a room full of rubbish? Most of all, where was the girl, whether her name was Janis or Esther or Jean? To my relief, Lisbeth dismissed Alfred and me as soon as we got back. My relief was short-lived.

'Back here at nine in the morning,' she said, her tone leaving no room for negotiation. 'You're going back up there.'

Sometimes, on Christmas Eve, if there is nothing pressing, I could switch off from work early enough to watch *Hercule Poirot's Christmas* while wrapping presents. Not tonight. I just sat with my unanswered questions.

·   ·   ·

ARMED with his camera and annoying enthusiasm, Alfred accompanied me back to East Docks the next morning. I almost expected BMX girl to be sitting there, ready to tell all, but that was not to be. When I rapped on the door, to my surprise, it swung open. No-one here at all.

Inside, the sitting room was as it had been the night before. Moving cautiously, I headed for the garage entrance. If I expected that to be the same, I was wrong. It was almost empty: all the junk that had littered the place - the old chair, the kids' toys, the books - all gone. When I went back in, I saw something: a Christmas card, opened, on the table. On the inside of the Season's Greetings Glittery Robin, no name, just a drawing: a riderless BMX bike, with a smiley below it. I suspected I had been conned, but apart from that, nothing made sense.

MUM AND DAD and I were having our annual Christmas dispute about watching The Queen. 'Not in my flat, never,' I argued, with Dad backing me up. Then my mobile went. A voice identifying himself as a Met Inspector ordered me to be ready in twenty minutes. A car would pick me up and take me to Police Headquarters at Peel Street. I was told I would be there for some while. An inspector, from the Met? What was he doing here, far beyond his jurisdiction? Sure enough, an unmarked car arrived on time, then took me via Alfred's house to the centre of the city. Alfred, without explanation, had been told to bring his camera.

Our police escort took us to the fourth floor, where we were left for more than an hour, rather defeating the point of all the haste. The meeting room was equipped with best quality computers, a machine which looked like an overhead projector, and a screen. Some time later, WPC Laura Watson arrived, looking as worried as I was feeling. None of us spoke, probably fearing the room was bugged.

I recognised the Met Inspector's obnoxious voice when he entered. His looks matched his tone. 'Fat, sleazy, arrogant tosspot' were the words which came to me. He looked like Philip Glenister's character in *Life on Mars*, complete with camel coat and sneer. As though he read my mind, he turned on me and began his questioning. I went over the details of my investigation into Janis Beverley. He made no comment on my story, except to squash me when I asked what this was about. Before he interviewed Alfred, he removed the SWD camera and had it collected by a uniformed constable. First Laura, then Albert gave their versions. Twenty minutes later, a different policeman returned with a folder, probably containing prints of Alfred's pictures. The inspector took over, and, like a Metropolitan police version of Hercule Poirot, began revealing all.

'Recognise this man?' he asked, placing an A4 glossy photo of someone I had never seen. I said so. 'Picture him with a full white beard, white hair. See it?'

'Could be anyone with that description. Maybe Santa?' I said, just to annoy him, but I knew what he was getting at. Was this Mister Kennedy from 163? I was told to stop being a smart-arse.

'What about him?' he asked, placing a photo of the same man beside the first. I told him they were the same.

'Look again,' he said. Certainly, in the second picture, the subject was slightly different.

'He's had his nose broken in this one,' I said, eyes close to the table.

'He's had his nose broken by this guy in the other picture. His brother,' the Inspector said. So, two brothers, possibly twins.

'Who are they?' Laura asked, standing at my shoulder.

'Take you pick: Simpson, Beverley, Frizzell, Kennedy, or a dozen other names,' the man said. 'One of them was the old man at the flat, for sure. Now, look at this photo.' With a flourish, like the Belgian 'tec himself, he put a last picture on the table. 'Recognise the T-shirt? The logo?'

After a second, the three of us – Laura, Alfred, and I answered together: *Antiques Roadshow.*

'*Antiques Roadshow,*' the Inspector said with a nod, sounding like he'd just thrashed us on the X Box. 'And this guy – one of them at least – as Dominic Frizzell, drove a pantechnicon for the programme for months last year. While we're waiting on our antiques expert to arrive from the airport, I suppose I should read you three your rights, since I could charge you all with reset, handling stolen goods, accessories after the fact. Or just bleeding stupidity.'

After the smug bastard had left the room, we were stunned. A uniformed constable brought in polystyrene cups of thick, brown sludge, accompanied by a plate of madeleines. Alfred slurped and crunched his way through his share with vigour, while Laura and I sat with our own thoughts. After an hour, which felt like five, the door opened to admit our Metropolitan friend and two women, one about my age, the other only twenty. The inspector cut short the introductions, saying only that the younger woman was a curator of some museum, while the other worked for Lloyd's Insurers.

'These ladies are going to have a look at the photographs from the garage; you lot might try to figure out what happened while they do so,' the inspector said. For perhaps ten minutes, the two women, using magnifying glasses and jewellers' loupes, muttered to themselves, to each other, making notes the whole time. When they straightened up, the older woman smiled, as though apologising for what she was about to say.

'During the filming of this season, The *Antiques Roadshow* production team has suffered some losses. High value items which disappeared during shooting. Following an investigation by our agents, Lloyd's has determined that carefully planned thefts took place in various locations. Suspicion fell on a driver, Dominic Frizell.'

The younger woman now spoke. 'The items in question are clearly visible in these pictures of the garage you raided.'

'Junk, we thought?' Alfred asked. The women shook their heads and offered us their magnifying glasses. That they showed no sign of smugness endeared them to me. The younger woman took a Sharpie and drew a circle round the tarpaulin covered chair.

'What you are looking at there is a Thomas Chippendale chair, with original covering, stolen from Newby Hall, which houses the only collection of these chairs known to exist.'

Her colleague looked at her notebook before speaking. 'Value: almost incalculable. At least half a million pounds.' Back to the curator.

'Here, on the bench, an original Superman comic. The very first appearance of Clark Kent and Jor El. The only copy ever to be auctioned fetched $32 million. This one was stolen from a collection at The Duke of Athol's castle.'

'And we were going to wrap stuff in it,' Alfred chirped.

'And finally,' the Lloyd's lady said, 'the marbles game. Do you notice anything about this set, constable?'

Laura peered through the offered jeweller's loupe, then straightened up. 'That big yellow bool in the middle; it's well, bigger than the others.'

The young woman, with awe in her voice, whispered.

'You are looking at a pearl, not from an oyster, but from a very rare South Asia snail. Formed in the same way as oyster pearls, but much, much more valuable, because of their rarity. They are Melo Melo pearls, and that one is unique.'

The insurance woman went on. 'The value of Melo Melo pearls depends on colour – in this case deep yellow – and the fire inside. Some go for three million pounds, some more. With this one, a perfect pearl, just keep adding noughts to the value till you run out of ink.'

'For a big yellow bool?' I asked, equally awed.

It was time for the sneering Inspector to reveal all.

'What we think happened is that the driver, having distracted the production team somehow, stashed one of these each trip. It might take the curator at each venue days, sometimes weeks, to discover the theft. We have stills of each of the targeted venues, but no idea how the theft was managed. Maybe there was an accomplice. Anyway, the villain smuggled his pieces in a false bottom in the van, then moved it on to a house in Corby, where we almost caught up with them. They ended up in Scotland, possibly to divide up the loot. But we think there was a falling out among thieves. One brother, double-crossing the other, had barricaded the stuff in that garage, probably while he arranged transportation out of the country. The other brother, unable to get at the goods, came up with this trick to get the gear. Get an investigation going, force the Fire Service to break open the barriers, then skip off with the loot, while the other brother is sorely out of pocket.'

'Bastards!' I muttered. They had used us in an elaborate plot to bust open Aladdin's cave. Unaccountably, Alfred asked to see the stills of the *Antiques Roadshow* programmes. He bent over the table, straightened, bent over again, then nudged me. I gasped. I saw what he did.

Borrowing the Sharpie, I began circling the photos. 'Look there,' I said, glad to have a shot at my own Poirot moment. 'And there, and there.'

In each photo, one of the Roadshow presenters was talking to camera; a young girl gazed attentively in each photo. In some, her hair was blonde, in others, auburn, in others black. But always there with a tail of hair tied with a blue ribbon. BMX girl. The accomplice. Used to distract the presenter while Dominic Frizzell – probably her dad – made the theft.

As I suspected at the start, I spent my festive period writing report after report about BXM girl, her father, and her uncle. One of them, doubtless scouring the world for his dysfunctional family and his cut of the goods. I sometimes imagine BMX girl in the Bahamas, or Hawaii, or Caracas, scooting around the streets on a top of the range bike, wearing a choker with a big yellow bool at her throat.

Then came the summons.

Starting my defence, I began with what sounded like the opening of a joke:

'There were these two pythons...'

THREE ELDERLY MAIDS

It is difficult to seethe in the auditorium of a proscenium arch theatre. Hardwood seatbacks restrict restless movement of the knees, which, in my case, is a requirement for effective seething. But I was bubbling nicely. Watching the trio of fifty-year-olds sing *Three Little Maids from School* was beyond absurd. It was grotesque. Their singing betrayed the decayed vocal cords of women of a certain age; the varicose veins and arthritic knees inhibited their approximation of choreography. Instead of skipping like three sixteen-year-old Japanese girls, they looked more like three octogenarians unable to locate their Zimmers.

'Enchanting, n'est-ce pas?' giggled the strange little chap who had insinuated himself into the red velvet seat beside me. I glanced at him, wondering whether he was being sarcastic.

'What stage presence. What beautiful top notes. Nothing to beat the vocality of the mature soprano, don't you think?' he went on. Apparently, he was neither sarcastic nor a music lover.

I tried to constrict my eardrums — physically impossible,

of course — to block the wailing of the trio. Their shredding of the last notes: *Three little maids... from school*, caused me to screw up my eyes. My companion was blind and deaf, since he did not notice the grimace that accompanied my internal shriek.

'Bravo Jackie, Elspeth, Beverly. Bravo. Encore.'

Beverly, playing the lead, Yum Yum, gave what might have been an appreciative curtsey before needing the support of her fellow maidens to straighten up. Looking more like Hattie Jacques than a svelte sixteen-year-old Asian lassie, Bev weighed in at fifteen stones. Quite how she might fit into a kimono without appearing like a hippo in a tent I did not know. At least it would hide the lumpy knees and varicose veins. Assuming my companion was a relative of one of the offending singers, I stared at him. I also looked around for the director of this company, whom I had yet to meet. As I turned back to him, I saw with fascination that he had turned his attention to a box of Liquorice Allsorts. He was nibbling the bobbly bits of the round blue one with great attention to detail. The action gave him the appearance of a squirrel. He introduced himself.

'Pardon, mam'selle,' he said, through tiny blue bobbly bits, some of which exploded onto my cardigan with his plosives. 'Gerard Antrobus, Gerry, to my many friends. I have the honour of being impresario and director of this company. You must be...?'

'Katherine, Mister Antrobus,' I nodded, my spirit dropping with rapidity. Surely squirrel-man could not be the director my friend had sent me to meet.

'Yes, yes, yes, yes, yes. Welcome to our ménage, Kitty. You are most welcome, chérie.'

Mister Antrobus set a record then, for being offensively stupid in the fewest number of sentences. He enjoyed the performance of the three little blimps from school; he spoke in schoolboy French; he chewed sweeties in the most irritating and dribbly way; finally, he called me 'Kitty'.

'Let us away to that most sacred of places, Mam'selle Kitty, the stage of any theatre,' he purred. For the first time, I agreed with him. A theatre stage is sacred. We climbed the steps through the orchestra pit and took our place, ominously, stage left, whence devils and villains make their entrance.

'Ladies, ladies, ladies, let me introduce Kitty Winters, a gift from our friend, Mark Broadley, from The School.' Before I could correct him on both my names, he went on. 'Mark commends her as a useful addition to our company. He recommends we take her to our collective bosoms.'

I stepped across the stage where the three singers – an imposing collective bosom indeed – had recently shredded one of Sullivan's finest pieces. With the reluctance of people asked to touch a leper, Jackie, Elspeth, and Beverly shook my hand.

'Perhaps you might favour us with something from *The Mikado*? Do you know anything of this score?' Antrobus asked.

'I have sung Yum Yum before, Gerry,' I answered. 'Also, Annie Oakley, Sister Sara and Guinevere.' It was the turn of the three hippos to seethe. I could almost see speech bubbles above their heads reading *Uppity Bitch*.

'Mrs Antrobus, my darling, would you tinkle us out a tune from the score? Shall we say…?'

'*The Sun Whose Rays*', I said, speaking now to the accompanist, whom I assumed was the spouse of the director. I deduced a degree of nepotism was involved in her choice as pianist, since her average was to hit two notes out of three with any accuracy. The song I had requested was the heroine's first song in Act Two, possibly the most beautiful in the whole operetta. Once again, she murdered the intro.

I sang beautifully. Like many aspiring actresses, I have little trouble with my ego: I know I sing beautifully. As well as a rich, powerful voice with excellent range, I also have dramatic talent, something unique in this assembly so far today. I have a figure which shows well on stage. Indeed, in *Annie Get Your Gun*, I made a striking, sexy Sioux Indian at the end of Act One. Most of the male cast – the straight ones – and all the stage crew pursued me to my wigwam. I enjoyed the attention. By the end of the song, which I rescued from Mrs Antrobus by singing over her terrible fingering, I should have won over my hearers. The director, sitting in a wobbly lotus position on the footlights, was sucking a liquorice pipe.

The conversation from my three rivals was deliberately sotto voce, designed to allow me to hear.

'Thin, reedy singing,' Jackie said in an audible stage whisper. 'Terrible register and no definition.'

'The phrasing was all wrong,' continued Elspeth.

'Her looks are all bad. Immature,' Beverly, the leader of the threesome, concluded.

'All righty, ladies… and gentlemen. If we might assemble to discuss interpretation and casting of this most magical of operas, this incredibly unique score and libretto,' Gerry trilled.

The impresario's negative tally was mounting in my mind. Fearing that I would betray my annoyance, or possibly display my secret speech bubble, I buried my face in a hankie. I could hear myself screaming inside: *The Mikado* is an operetta, not an opera, and something cannot be incredibly unique – it's either unique, or it's not. I should not have come. Liquorice Man arranged a wide semi-circle of seats, with himself facing twenty would-be thespians. One of the three men present shifted his chair to beside mine and cocked his head sideways, effectively shutting out all the rest.

'Harry,' he said, offering to elbow bump me. 'Harry Belling, tenor, teacher, and another interloper here.'

I put him at thirty years of age, with a broad, open face, blue eyes capable of sarcasm, and a mighty high opinion of himself. Reciprocating his air-elbow-bump, I introduced myself as Katherine. As our director giggled and ingratiated himself with the assembled *chéres madames*, I chatted with the tenor.

'Why are you here, Katherine?' he asked, an exaggerated frown on his brow.

'Strange question,' I answered. 'We're all here for the same reason, aren't we?' He scoffed, using a combination of blown raspberry and head shake.

'I've seen you, Katherine,' he said. 'In *Guys and Dolls*. Sister Sara. An amateur production. You are wasting your time auditioning here. Three things: you can sing; you're an actor; and you're younger, with nice legs. Madame Mimm and co will never let you be cast in a principal role. They run this 'company', intimidating director Gerry.'

'Thanks for the confidence boost, mister,' I said. 'Why are you here?'

'*A wand'ring minstrel I, a thing of...* I'm the only guy who can almost hit the notes. I'm supposed to be singing Nanki Poo.'

'Well, Nanki, I've left Redroofs Theatre School, and I'm open to offers. I've an audition coming up next week. But just in case...'

My new friend nodded. 'As many irons in the theatrical fire as possible. Quite right. What's the audition for?'

'It's a disaster movie. Not much hope of getting the part, but who knows? I love Gilbert and Sullivan, anyway.'

The impresario called the cast together by shaking his sweetie box like a pair of maracas.

'Now then, fellow thespians, attention if you please. First, let me thank you all. What a splendid turnout. Plenty of seasoned professionals to form the spine of the production. Also, one or two fresh faces to be added as choristers.'

I watched Beverly mouth the word *Chorus* to the other maids. By now, I was regretting taking up Mark Broadley's introduction. I had served my time as a member of various choruses; I had no wish to do so again. Certainly not as second violin to any of this lot.

'Before we come to the casting, one or two words about my interpretation of the libretto,' Gerry said, by now reduced to sucking on a liquorice shoelace. He stretched this strand of black sweetie too tightly, resulting in his being smacked in the face when it whiplashed across him. The liquorice stripe on his right cheek gave him a funky look, though.

'As has been wisely put to me – and my thanks to Beverley for her common sense – the story revolves around a travelling musician pursuing a Japanese schoolgirl. Perhaps when written, this would have been acceptable, but now, it is most certainly NOT acceptable.' Smiles from the members of the coven.

'Excuse me, Gerry,' my companion said, edging forward in his seat. 'You're not serious? *The Mikado* has been performed without any hint of sleaze for over a hundred years.'

'Certainly, we're serious, young man,' Beverly snapped. 'Just listen if you would be so kind.'

'A grown man kissing with a girl straight from school? If that's not seedy…' one of the others contributed.

'So,' Gerry went on, 'the story has been beautifully rewritten thus. Nanki Poo, disguised as a musician, is actually a heartbroken maiden pursuing the Lord High Executioner himself.' Stunned silence from everyone apart from Gerry and his coven. 'Again, my thanks to the multi-talented Beverley for her Dickensian writing.'

'Sorry to interrupt, Boss,' my friend said, his knees trembling in the beginnings of a seethe. 'I can't see myself cross-dressed trying to woo whichever elderly gent plays the Lord High whatnot.'

Another silence.

'Perhaps if we get to the casting, it might forestall further interruption, director,' Beverley contributed, lounging back in the manner of Rees-Mogg in parliament.

'Well, yes. Darling,' Mister Antrobus said, a smile across his liquorice striped visage. 'Yes. I will, as senior actor in the company, play Nanki Poo.'

He stressed the *OR* syllable in *act-OR*, like the Spitting Image version of a louche thespian. The guy was at least sixty years old, with the physical presence of a woodlouse, and the vocal timbre to match. I looked sideways at the ex-Nanki Poo. I was sure I saw him look about, no doubt searching for the nearest exit.

'The adorable Beverley will, of course, play Yum Yum,' he went on. 'Yum Yum by name, Yum Yum by nature,' he snickered. So it continued, with our impresario disposing of the principal parts to pre-existing members of the group.

'And me?' my new friend asked.

'Well, of course, we will need a strong gentlemen's chorus for this piece,' Gerry purred. The strong gentlemen's chorus seemed to be two ex-lollipop men, retired when their pole would no longer support them.

'What about Katherine here?' Harry asked, fighting my corner. Unnecessarily. I had already spied the nearest exit. 'The ladies' chorus for her? Or perhaps she should strengthen the male chorus, appearing in drag.'

The Boss ignored the sarcasm.

'No, no, no, no, no,' Gerry trilled. 'I wouldn't ask Kitty to join the chorus. An altogether more important role for her.' Dramatic pause.

'Prompter,' he went on, with a look with implied I should be eternally grateful. 'In the orchestra pit with the libretto; in case any of our troupe forgets their lines.'

'Pivotal,' Beverley mewed. 'She won't even have to learn the script.'

Smug smiles abound.

'Well,' I said, eyeing the stage door, the shortest distance to the street. 'I must forego that pivotal honour, I'm afraid, and in the words of the beauteous Julie Andrews: *So long, farewell, etc.*'

'Do svidaniya, comrades,' the former chorister added as he joined me in heading for the exit.

What the reaction was inside, I neither knew nor cared. Taking a deep breath to clear my lungs of the fustiness, I smiled at Harry.

'So, if I'm to recognise your name on a billboard, what'll it say?' he asked, before turning off in the opposite direction.

'Katherine. Kate, usually. Kate Winslet.'

GET A MESSAGE TO MY UNCLE

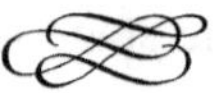

'*L*ady, are you are crying?'

Being hard with Sofia only satisfied my anger for moments. She was the nearest target to hand and would do.

'I never cry,' I said, without raising my head. 'Have you ever seen me cry?' Turning to face her, I felt even after crushing her with my tone, she was intruding by her presence. I threw the stylus, but she ducked. As she made to back out of my chamber, I softened my voice. I did not need to explain myself to her, yet she was too easy to hurt. And not the one I wanted to.

'To my uncle. I'm writing a message. And I never cry.'

The girl picked up the ivory stick and returned it, moving as quickly as her damaged foot allowed. Even the sound of her slipper as it dragged across the marble floor drove me to further rage. She limped out of the room, probably to forestall another display of temper.

What would I say to him? Perhaps if I described today's attack, he would react. Yet his reactions were always extreme. Did I really want that? But the time was coming when matters had to be resolved. Maybe I needed my uncle and his extreme reaction now. I knew today's incident would seem minor to those outside the palace: boys being crass and oafish. But I also knew that the time would soon come when this rough display would become serious, brutal, deadly. I also guessed that my uncle, the shrewdest of men, might anticipate civil war. Encourage it. I reviewed these events, at first in my head, then by scribing letters on the wax tablet.

It was Tolly's squeaking, hysterical voice that alerted me to trouble. That they sought me out in my bath was further cause for worry. If not today, then soon, these jackals would take advantage of my becoming a woman, and not just another plaything to be broken.

'She'll be in there!' my brother shrieked. His boldness and the hysteria in his voice told of a drinking session with his friends. Most of the household was absent for training; he would have known that too. The restraining presence of the older men had been removed. After pulling on leggings and a tunic, I looked for a jug or a vase, anything I could use as a weapon. My throat now throbbing, I found a fruit knife before discarding it. I didn't want to kill them. And yet. If I did, Tolly would be first to die; the others I would castrate. Instead, I grabbed a bowl of figs, which, though it would appear childish, might keep these fools off me.

Before I could reach the corridor, with its hidden passageway, my brother lurched into view. As I had guessed, he had been drinking, the purple stains on his tunic evidence that he often failed to find his mouth. And if he had been drinking, then he was drunk. He couldn't do it and stay human.

'Here she is, the beetle,' he laughed, in that vile snake's hiss.

As his two friends joined him, they, too, displayed his hysterical lack of decorum. They knew better than to approach me, but, like the hyenas they were, they followed the pack leader. Not because he was a natural leader, but because of who he was. He would give them licence to molest me.

'Here now, beetle, what are you doing with those figs? When we have wine for you - jugs, and jugs of it. Just like your father, a drunk. Used to lie in his own mess. Let's get you like that, eh?'

The first of the figs caught him in the chest. When I got my aim right, I hit him in the face, then several times in the groin. My brother's gross body obscured the others, following him. Now out of figs, my only chance, after throwing the bowl, was to run. Even although I was quicker than them, and immeasurably smarter, they were going to catch me. There was not enough room to stay out of their hands for long, so my brain had to take over from my legs. Feigning resignation, I laughed, although I saw the wicked intent in my brother's eyes.

'Tolly, you can't drink. Last month, eh? After the ceremony. Remember how you had to be put to bed, how the slaves threw the covers out in the morning because of the stains? And the smells. If you give me the ewer, I can get Sofia to mix...'

Although fat and inactive, my brother knew how to hit. The slap he delivered might have broken my jaw if I hadn't seen it coming. Even so, it took me off my feet.

'You keep that sad cripple out of my sight, or I'll take the toes of the other foot.'

Before I could roll away, his entire weight descended on me, knees pinning my shoulders to the cold marble. Tolly always appeared disgusting. His under garment was now close to my face, with its various shades of staining, his tunic reeking of syrupy sweat and rancid wine. With the repulsive saliva-streaked folds of fat round his chin and neck, he was a gargantuan nightmare. His two jackals, laughing, kept their distance. Everyone in Alexandria knew better than to offend me, so they made do with taunts and spits.

'Now, drink the wine, beetle. Your father bathed in it, drank it, and drowned in it.' He poured the vinegary stuff over my face, calling on the others to hold my mouth open. These two, however, saw not only the terror, but the anger for which I was already famous. They held back.

'Though we had different fathers, brother, they were both drunks. And you want to follow in their staggering foot-steps?' I asked. The wine stopped my speech. As it spattered over me, causing my nostrils to fill, I pouched a mouthful of the liquid, then spat it with venom into the gross face drooling above me. My strength comes from fury and savage instinct, making up for my lack of weight. I punched his groin, making him remove his knees. The other two backed off. As I squirmed to the side, I aimed a further blow with my right heel at the same place. With an explosive vomit, he rolled to the side and wailed, scattering his red-brown mess as he did so. The combination of sounds, smell and my fury resulted in the jackals' departure. Taking an expensive pottery jar, I threw it to the ground and picked up the longest shard.

'If you ever touch me again, half-brother, I will finish this job, and take pleasure in doing so,' I said, holding the edge against the throbbing blue vein, as thick as my thumb, in his neck. Before releasing him, I flicked the weapon against the vein, causing an immediate spurt of dark red blood. 'Take this and keep it there, or you will be dead in minutes,' I said, holding a cloth against the vein. 'I will send someone.'

If I wrote to my uncle, I knew what would happen. Though our fathers' wills made him our guardian and execu-tor, he might now give up trying to keep the peace. He would have to choose between us. And he favoured me. There was money involved, the wealth that came from Egypt's corn. Because I was not sure that I trusted my guardian not to take more than his share, I put off the decision. Although Tolly, as he reached manhood – at least physically – had become more openly hostile and aggressive, I had not thought the time was yet right to remove him. That we could not live in the same household had been obvious for months. The time was now, today. I needed more allies first, and I knew where I could find one.

'Barnabus, is it? That's your name?' I said, walking over to the bench near to where he was working as casually as I could under the circumstances. I knew I was pretty, have done since I was young. I also knew that soon I become desirable – within reason. There was too much strength in my jaw, too much intensity in my blue-black eyes. I would attract men, as I attracted boys, but there would always be a fear there. A voice in their heads: *There is danger in this one.* The gardener nodded, then bowed deep. There it was, that fear, when I ordered him to sit with me. I could see his embarrassment because of the dirt and sweat, signs that he was working hard. I told him so. As I toyed with the idea of teasing him, I heard a roaring from inside the house. No time for games.

'Barnabus, listen to me. I need help today. You know my brother, what he is like?' The boy hesitated, then nodded, looking over my shoulder, his eyes wide. He still had not spoken, but, in a surprising movement, he bared his upper right arm, revealing massive purple scarring, recent.

'Tolly?' I asked, knowing the answer. Without waiting, I went on. 'My brother has lost control of himself. I know he does that sometimes...' I touched his injured arm, causing a deep blush. 'This time, though, it is me he is looking for. He might kill me. I can hear him screaming for more of his pack to follow him. He is drunk, raging, and beyond reason.'

The noises within the house were now terrifying. My brother's voice had risen to an incoherent, deafening screech. The sounds of destruction were unmistakable, as was the noise of running feet, a sign that more and more were joining him. His mind, rarely in balance, had been tipped over the edge by my besting him.

'Barnabus, you have no reason to stand with me, although you have even less cause to love my brother. If you help me now…' As I searched for bribes and positions to promise him, he stood up. I noticed, as he towered above me, the strength in those shoulders and arms.

'I don't need a reason. Tell me what I can do, lady.'

'Indoors. If you can, get past them. Find Sofia. Tell her to get to my uncle, in the harbour. He will bring sailors from the ships and settle things until my brother recovers.'

'And you? If you stay here, they'll find you. I can fight them off.' The boy's impractical loyalty touched me, but even those broad shoulders and scarred arms would not hold ten or twenty drunken rioters, led by my insane half-brother.

'Just find Sofia. And when she brings my uncle, tell her I am in the passageway. She will know where.'

When he left, I looked around for any kind of weapon, for the second time today. I found a bronze statue of Mercury holding the rod of Caduceus. As I removed this staff, I smiled at the irony: this symbol of peace I was about to use as a lance to gut my brother and his friends. A sudden clattering noise. With my back against a pillar, I braced myself for the onslaught. Instead, the gardener re-appeared, wild-eyes and hysterical voice.

'She is gone,' he gasped. 'The kitchen workers think she ran away in case your brother does what he did to her before. And they're all now hiding or have run off. There's just you and me left, lady.'

I thought about asking him to race to the harbour to get

my uncle; it was too late for that. Tolly was leading his mob this way; there was little chance of the boy getting past them, and no chance he would bring my uncle in time. Though I admired my hero's bravery and strength, I doubted if he was quick of wits. Taking his hand, twice the size of my own and roughened, I led him to the entrance of the hidden passageway. My brother knew it existed, and would soon find it, but a few more minutes of life were worth having. Pulling aside the vine leaves, I squeezed behind the concealed wall, pulling Barnabus after me.

Moments later, further sounds of destruction, accompanied by the banging of pots and clashing of improvised weapons, echoed through my den. It seemed strange to me that, as I breathed the stale, mossy air in that confined space, my terror gave way to a momentary love of living. I did not regret what I would not fulfil, but instead enjoyed the enforced imprisonment and the presence of the earthy giant who would soon join me in death. I kissed him lightly on the neck. A battering on the walls began, as well as hoots and whistles from the wild animals outside.

'Beetle, Beetle. Time has come, little sister, for me to rid myself of the beetle. My friends have plans for you, but I will finish with you myself. Think about that, beetle.'

Then there was light, as the plasterwork covering the thin boards was smashed. Again and again, using pillars removed from the garden, the attackers shredded my flimsy walls. The light invaded my sanctuary, till, with a great crash, a whole panel collapsed. Shrieks and whistles proclaimed their triumph. There would be no restraint this time from these jackals. Guessing what their leader had in mind, there was no reason for holding back from the deadly fun. There would be an end now.

Still streaked with his own mess, my brother took my face in his gross, grey fingers.

'They might have made me marry you, you know.' He laughed, but his laughter did not last. He smashed his fist into my jaw, then straddled me.

'See this,' he said, pulling his under garment aside to reveal the fat, grey slug of his manhood. 'I would have forced this into you. And might yet.'

Through the blood from my mouth, and the tears I boasted I never shed, I saw my tormentor smashed to the marble by a white arm guard. My unseen saviour now placed a booted foot on Tolly's throat.

'Do not move, or I will crack your head like an eggshell beneath my foot.'. My brother's massive torso obscured the owner of the voice. But I recognised the speaker all the same. 'I should have dealt with this before.'

Although short in stature, there was no doubting the strength of the man now dominating the garden. Not just his broad shoulders, his muscular legs, his intimidating eyes, but him. His presence, as ever, held sway wherever he was. Behind him stood Sofia, shaking and gasping for breath. Around us, sailors from the Second Augusta seized the mob and methodically slit their throats.

'Uncle Gaius,' said Tolly, stepping back from me, eyes bulging.

'Your guardian, not your uncle. I am, however, executor of your father's estate. By the will of the Senate and the People of Rome, Ptolemy the Fifteenth is removed from succession. You must take exile well beyond these shores. If we meet again, it will be the last day you see.

'And you,' he went on, helping me to my feet. 'Though you look like a meretrix who lost a brawl in some low taberna, you are daughter of Isis, ruler of the Upper and Lower Nile. Cleopatra the Fourth, Queen of Egypt.'

THE CLOCKS STOP

*N*ew teacher today. History. Thinks he's a hunk. LOL.
I have got into the habit of sending Halle texts, even though I don't need to. She knows my thoughts as quickly as I have them. That's the way it is with us. Although the tutor was a phony, I enjoyed History. I knew we could have a lot of fun with this one; more that we usually have with new staff. They'd have warned him about us, for sure. But when new teachers try to work us out, it's even more fun in the end. I've even seen some of them making notes as they think they can tell us apart. We would certainly have fun with Mister Hopkins. But there was the name: M. Hopkins.

'He thought my name was funny, when I told him you spell it with an H,' I said to Halle. Most times, it's difficult to know whether we're speaking aloud, since we don't need to. This night, I think we did.

'But you told him why,' Halle said. 'The story about Dad working in the office in Cairo. I can hear you, in your I'm a nice little kitten voice. *It's not Ella, sir, it's Ellah* – emphasis on the 'ah' – *a North African spelling. It rhymes with Allah and means little fairy.*' We spluttered our Slush Puppies at her impersonation of my Little Kitten voice.

'The others in Geography heard he looks like Johnny Depp. I saw him on the stairs, with the swept back hair and wee black beard. Slouches, and walks with his bum. He seems like a tosser,' Halle said, as always, right about people.

'For sure,' I said. 'But he's new, so let's give him time, eh?'

'Not a chance,' Halle said, feeling my sarcasm. 'Tomorrow, we'll switch.' She stopped then, sensing the darkness in my mind. We think in layers. 'You think there's more? Not just... It's like Miss Proctor? You do. It's the name, isn't it?'

'We'll fix the hair and clothes in the morning before we switch for the day. See if you agree with me,' I said, louder than I meant. Even when we do speak, it's in whispers. We decided even before we learned to talk, not to let others hear us. She knew –and felt – how strong my sense of this guy was.

All identical twins switch. School, parties, boyfriends. The nuisance is changing the parting and fringes. The hair never quite sits right, but then we're critical; no-one else notices. The collar badges and scrunchies are easy enough, as is the change of tights and shoes. We worked it out by Primary Two: if you want to make a twins-switch, most of the time you dress differently, so that, when you change over, the teachers are fooled. Miss Proctor, though, she saw our eyes.

Miss Proctor saw it just before the end. Strange coincidence, a Miss Proctor coming here to teach in Primary School. From Salem, Boston, Mass. Just like the one in the witch trials. Our kind do not believe in coincidences. And we know we are always hunted. She was the only person, apart from Mum and Dad, who saw it, and, even then, I think poor father humoured my mother. They both realised what we were before we knew. Or rather, we always knew, we just didn't have the words to express it. Mum first, of course, but then she would realize it, wouldn't she?

While identical twins are uncommon, mirror-image twins are super-rare. And Halle and I are unique. I remember the day Miss Proctor looked into my eyes. Eyes wide, mouth open, a quick hand to the throat; the way you know someone has seen something that terrifies them. Her mouth slackened, her breathing quickened, she choked, trying to speak. She had noticed our mirror-image-ness, even though Halle and I were in different classes. If we sit together, it's easier to spot. Where she's right, I'm left. I'm always left. Hair parting, writing with opposite hands, folding arms, crossing legs, alway the opposite to the other.

It wasn't just the eyes that Miss Proctor recognised; she was the only person, apart from mother, who saw what we were. What I remember of that day is Miss Proctor explaining, in her New England accent, Latin words which are the same in English: *dictator*, for example. Then she came to *sinister*. She explained that was the Latin word for left, and that people used to believe that left-handed people were sinister, dangerous. Witches, even. Before she laughed it off, she looked into my eyes, and she saw it. Sinister. I felt her terror. Maybe she noticed our eyes. If she did, she can't have told anyone since nothing happened. No-one would have believed her. Halle with a blue left eye and a grey right eye; with me, it's the opposite. But even that wasn't it. She saw what we were. What she read in my eyes that day – centuries of wickedness and persecution – turned her guts inside out. I felt it and knew we must act. Water under the bridge, literally.

I replayed the Proctor ending in my mind the same night I met Mister Hopkins. I heard the certainty of my ancestors' voices on the day I saw him and learned his name. Although I went to Geography next day, I was listening to Halle in the

History class. Hopkins, in fashionable white tailored shirt, slacks, and loafers, thought he was Tom Cruise. He sat on the edge of his desk while the daft girls texted their friends about him. But Halle noticed what I had. She saw the coming fog, like the blue-black clouds that gather in cheap CGI movies, accompanied by sinister music, foreshadowing danger. She could see it; I could feel it.

Because I was only half listening in Geography, we both had to write up notes about tectonic plates in South America. Not wishing to give ourselves away, we catch up with work on the day of a switch. She handed me today's notes from Hopkins. Although Halle tried to shield her mind, she real-ized I would react when I saw the next topic in History. Though she sat with maps of the Chile-Argentina border, she knew there was no point starting. Anticipating my volcanic eruption, she was not disappointed.

Her notes turned to ashes in my hands, so hot did they become. 'King James. The Scottish Witch Trials! How did you keep that from me all day? You know where this'll go, don't you?' This time I did raise my voice, unnecessarily. We are never out of tune, so why did she keep this from me? And how? The air in our bedroom turned sulphurous.

'Because I knew you would explode, I tried to close off my mind. But it didn't work, not really. You've been in a mood since I was in History. The school clocks all stopped at eleven. That's a giveaway, sister.'

WE DIDN'T HAVE History the next day, so Halle and I went about business as normal: keeping distance between us, going to classes, listening to the crass stupidity of acned boys. They were all trying to impress Susie Chen, newly arrived from Hong Kong, and looking like Cho from *Harry Potter*. My gran sometimes used the expression 'someone's ears burning,' meaning they were being talked about. If texts do that, Hopkins would have needed earmuffs to cover his pink lobes. The only topic on social media among girls was the new History hunk. Both my sister and I agreed his nasal voice and choice of handouts made him Professor Bore, but that didn't stop the false lash flutterers. And he just loved it, I thought. I noticed the P.E. teacher bouncing along the corridor, lapping at his every syllable.

By the third day in his class, I was sure he was fake. For a start, nobody with a teaching degree could be that shallow. I considered what he might be hiding, other than what I assumed he was: another Miss Proctor. A finder, like her. I wondered if he was gay, which would have been a relief, since it meant my worst suspicion was wrong. But from the amorous verbal serve-and-volley with Miss Gymslip, that seemed wrong. He didn't appear to have a great depth to his subject knowledge, so perhaps he was just a rotten teacher. But – and this worried me most – he didn't once look me in the eye. Both Halle and I are pretty; it is unusual not to be looked at.

'We'll have to find out,' I whispered in my sister's head that Saturday night. As she often does when she is thinking, she sat with her legs straight up the wall above her headboard. Dangling my arms and head over the end of my bed, I heard her in my head.

'Will we have to leave, if you're right? Or can you fix it, like Miss Proctor?' Halle asked.

'We didn't have to move then; we were younger – presumed innocents – and one day she just didn't turn up. A drowning accident. We might need to be cleverer because more people are wary of us.'

'Don't let the clocks stop, though,' Halle said, drawing an invisible clock face on the wall with her right toes. 'You've got a plan, haven't you?'

. . .

I WANTED to fix it before Hopkins fully explored the topic of King James and the Scottish Witch Trials. The teacher had just reached the point when the king went to collect his bride.

'When King James was delayed by storms, bringing his new wife Anne back from Denmark, he was told witches sailed from North Berwick in a sieve to bewitch the waves. Shakespeare mentions this in *Macbeth*,' he said. This was my chance to prove myself right. I began to sing, but in my head.

> *In a sieve I'll thither sail*
> *And like a rat without a tail,*
> *I'll do, I'll do, and I'll do.*

HAD HE HEARD MY SONG? If he did, he gave no sign. Yet I'll swear he heard it. He was just good; that's why he was sent to find us. The rest of the class left. The clock, my Apple Watch, and his, no doubt, all stopped.

'You're English, aren't you, Mister Hopkins?' I asked. It was quite usual for girls to loiter at his desk, so there seemed nothing amiss with my doing so.

'Yes, that's right,' he said, smiling, but looking at the lump of jotters on his desk, not at me.

'Are you from Ipswich, maybe?' I went on. 'Only I've got cousins there.'

'Yorkshire, Harrogate, I'm afraid. Long way from East Anglia.'

'My family tree shows I had lots of ancestors, from there, all the way to Devon. But they died out centuries ago, sir. I think they drowned some of them as witches.'

Once again, there was nothing, no reaction. But he didn't

look me in the eye, not once. The clocks started again as I left.

'I HAD your man for Maths today,' Halle said, 'a please-take.' Tonight, she was practising a neck stand against the wall, while I lotussed on the floor. 'He's boring, sure enough. I'm not certain if that makes him a descendant of the Matthew Hopkins, Witchfinder General. Maybe the M. doesn't even stand for Matthew.'

Unusually, our thoughts criss-crossed, the same as the tangle Christmas fairy lights get into. Because she was right to my left, although in extremis she was as lethal as me, she could be more generous. Like now. She flopped down onto her Vikings duvet, breathing in my determination.

'I spoke about Anglia, about Devon; he must have known I was talking about Witchfinder Hopkins and about the three hundred he murdered there. I could feel the ancient prick-ings, the drownings. The water suffocated me today; the needles lanced me today. Look at the blood.' I showed her my arms, marked like stigmata. She had felt the stabbings when I had. 'He couldn't look me in the eye.' I unfolded my legs, stood up, and sang, misquoting Shakespeare, as I revolved anti-clockwise, contrary to nature, widdershins. Sinister.

By the pricking of my thumbs,
Through the years, my vengeance comes...
Minute after hour, slower and slower, always widder-shins, I drew her in.

FRIDAY AFTERNOON, last period, was the moment. His room was at the far end of the corridor, with only the fire exit beyond. The irony of the fire exit amused me. No-one would be along until the janitor did his closing up about five. Once our class was gone, there would just be me. Since he thought the room was empty, he jumped when I spoke.

'Ella', he said, 'It's nearly four.' He mispronounced my name again, leaving out the 'H.' To most people, it sounds the same, but I can tell. He looked up at the wall. 'That clock's stopped. The second time this week that's happened.'

'Have you ever heard of Matthew Hopkins, sir?' I asked, my Little Kitten voice back. 'He was called the Witchfinder General, in King James's time.'

'No relation of mine, I'm sure,' he said, switching off the whiteboard and giving me hints to leave. But he was determined not to look me in the eye.

'But if he had been, sir, and if you came from East Anglia, or Devon, he might be an ancestor of yours.' He still didn't look me in the eye.

'The trouble with witch-finders, sir, is that they don't know what to do when they find a real witch.' With his back turned to me, he did not see my fingers grow longer and longer and longer. They wrapped around his throat and stopped his own clock.

I looked down at the body, thinking that he was handsome. When he was alive. When I took the pile of handouts on the Scottish Witch Trials from his desk, they glowed hot in my hands, then fired the room as I scattered them.

The clock restarted just as I left through the fire exit.

Though churches are not our favourite places to visit, Halle and I both went to the memorial later in the month. It surprised me when the Head gave permission for Desmond Smythe, a friend of Mister Hopkins, to give a eulogy; perhaps she didn't know what he was, or what he would say. She introduced him as a Scottish artist of some renown. For a funeral service, he was certainly dressed flamboyantly, almost garishly.

'Mister Hopkins, as you knew him, was a teacher here for a brief time before the tragic fire that took his life. Maurice Hopkins was not my just friend; he was my partner. He was a very loving person who would have given so much to your school community had he lived. What most who met him did not realise was that he was the most intensely private, introverted man who became a teacher, hoping to overcome his shyness. When I first met him, he could not even meet my eyes. That's the kind of man Maurice was.'

Halle's voice giggled in my head. 'So, not Matthew Hopkins then, but Maurice. Phony only as a cover for being gay. Not a witch hunter, just a shy bloke who couldn't look people in the eye. Pity about the fire, then.' She finished with another giggle. We never feel regret. It isn't in us.

I shrugged back my answer to her mind. 'True enough, but he was still a rotten teacher.'

SHE SHOULDN'T HAVE MENTIONED THE BIKE

Department of Clinical Psychology, Edinburgh University

FROM: Elizabeth Menzies, B. Sc. Ph.D. Psy.D.
To: Lord Justice Clerk
cc: Procurator Fiscal, Crown Office and Procurator Fiscal Service. Hector Willoughby, DMBSCH.
Subject: Catherine Montague
June 9th

FURTHER TO A REQUEST from the Procurator Fiscal, I accepted the task of assessing the subject Catherine Montague, prior to her commitment for trial on two counts of murder, and one count of manslaughter. Having ten years' experience assessing those accused of serious crimes did not prepare me for the unique challenge I faced. The most significant aspect of my report is to be found in Appendix 1, the subject's statement. That this testimony was given through the use of hypnotherapy may present legal difficulties. The assignment required the use of this process.

Important Note: The following Section A, of necessity, is written using the terminology of professional psychotherapy. For a less technical explanation, please refer to section B.

A The immediate difficulty was that already faced by the investigating detectives: Catherine Montague being comatose following the RTA rendered her impossible to interview. Following her recovery from a medically induced coma, she remained incommunicable. Despite repeated interviews by investigating officers, she failed to answer questions. Medical tests on her vocal apparatus were inconclusive, although there seemed to be no obvious physical damage from the crash. Nursing staff reported she made noises during sleep, suggesting that either she deliberately refused to speak, or else suffered a form of traumatic amnesia. This, I now believe to be the case. Traumatic amnesias are psychological consequences of traumatic events: in this case, the car crash and actions preceding it. Dissociative psycho-traumatic mechanisms prevent the sufferer from reliving the trauma, resulting in loss of memory.

B WHAT THIS MEANS, in lay terms, is that a person who has suffered from a violent action subconsciously refuses to remember that action. The violent action here being both the car crash and the events preceding it. What is unusual – in fact unique to this case – is that the sufferer is usually the victim, and not the perpetrator, Ms. Montague. I had to determine whether Ms. Montague was feigning amnesia, or whether she was genuinely suffering complete memory loss.

C Unable to proceed, I decided to contact Doctor Hector Willoughby, senior member of the British Society of Clinical Hypnotists. In consultation with Ms. Montague's lawyer, he undertook three sessions with her, using hypnosis to awaken her memory of events of 10th May this year. These sessions took place in the presence of Ms. Montague's lawyer, on the understanding that anything revealed during this process would be submitted to Lord Justice Clark for a legal ruling on admissibility in court.

D Doctor Willoughby's report – a transcript of Ms. Montague's statement under hypnosis – is submitted under Stage Three of Forensic Psychologist's Late Disclosure Evidence.

E Police statement of evidence is presented in Appendix 2.

Appendix 1

THE FOLLOWING IS the transcript of a statement given by Catherine Montague, under clinical hypnosis, on 16th May 2020. Those present: Catherine Montague, Elizabeth Menzies (Forensic Psychologist), Dr. Hector Willoughby (Clinical Hypnotist), Jennifer Korda (Lawyer representing Ms. Montague).

MOTHER DIDN'T COMPARE us with each other. Nor did Father. Not openly, anyway. They knew we were different. I realized I was clever from early on. Primary school thought I was special. They gave mother a book called *Bringing up the Gifted Child,* which I read but she didn't. When Cecilia came along, she was 'loved for herself.' That meant they recognized she wasn't another prodigy, but they would make up for it by being even nicer to her. They all did. When I think about it, I suppose hatred is inherent in our family genes.

Mother and Father were a pretty strange pair. Not really a couple. She said she was a feminist; Dad just liked women. They both appreciated old music, like Ella Fitzgerald and Bing Crosby. Mother caused a fuss at the PTA in my primary school because they had a book called *The Catcher on the Rye* in the library. Lots of swearing and sex in it, she said, so they banned it. No-one read it, anyway, because it was too hard for primary kids. I took it out of the local library and read it in Primary Five. Mother was a maths teacher and fanatical golfer. She was bad at the sums, good with clubs.

She almost made the Scottish Ladies team once. That was the year she caused trouble in her school. By insisting that the male staff allow her to play in the Men's Golf Outing, she had the tournament cancelled when all the men withdrew. I thought it was strange that she liked almost being selected for the Scottish Ladies but objected to men's golf outings. Even at that age, I recognised the absurdity of accepting women only events but objecting to men-only events. Father pretended to read *The Times* and looked at *The Sun* when Mother wasn't there. So, he ogled often. He told dirty jokes to my uncles and put his arm round my aunts' waists when he could.

It was always a matter of competition with us. Because I was so clever, I didn't need toys and childish books and comics. Mother and Father convinced the wider family that I would appreciate *Science & Technology* and *National Geographic*, but not *The Bunty*. Isn't it funny how parents never really get their children, especially when they're girls? The teachers at primary school were always careful not to compare us, but don't think they didn't make up for Cecilia being a normal pupil. Cecilia was *Polite Pupil of the Year, Girl-Most-Likely-to-be-Invited-to-a-Party*, and *Cute Burd of the School.* I made up that last one.

It was Uncle Bernard who made the thoughtless comparison on the Christmas when we got the bikes. "This is Catherine, the clever one, isn't it? And that's little Celia, that plays the recorder," he said. While the other uncles laughed, my sister looked at them and whispered through her braced teeth, "Cecilia." The bikes we got were different, too. Mine was a black and gold Raleigh racing machine, which I never could go. Cecilia's was a pink *Lazytown* bike. There were ribbons on the high handlebars, a pink glittery seat, and decals of Stephanie and Sportacus. Cecilia managed to race my Raleigh surprisingly well, surprisingly quickly. When I went to try her Stephanie bike, I always found it locked – with a Robbie Rotten padlock.

In school, when my sister she finished her work, they gave her *The Beano* and *The Lazytown Annual* to read. *Lord of the Flies* is what I got. Don't get me wrong, I quite liked *Lord of the Flies,* because I could imagine myself killing Piggy. My parents decided I was so clever that I should be sent to a fee-paying school in Aberdeen. They sent me there in what would have been my sixth year of primary schooling, while Cecilia continued where she was. I spent weekends at home when Cecilia and I caught up on family gossip. In particular, she informed me that all was not well there: Father had put one too many arms round one too many aunts at Easter and had been given his marching orders. She took him back later but sent him to the attic to live. Mother invited a counsellor to stay. She became a counsellor of the bedchamber, and a noisy one at that. Once again, because I was the clever one, no-one bothered to counsel me, though Cecilia got lots of attention. And presents.

I left school, went to Oxford, graduated, and became a doctor, living in Morningside, Edinburgh. So one night, whatever the date was, I got a phone call which surprised me. It was Cecilia, whom I hadn't seen or heard from since she went off to be a hippy three years before. I was in the kitchen preparing a Greek salad with my friend Elena, who was taking me to the ballet.

It surprised Elena I had a sister, since I had never mentioned her. I remember what I said then: 'I don't have a sister. We divorced years ago.' Clever answer, wasn't it? I went on to say mine was a dysfunctional family, all divorced from each another. Before Cecilia appeared, I explained the twisted relationship I had with my sister, so that, in the event of a bust-up, Elena would not be shocked.

The provocation started on the threshold. She arrived with an old boyfriend of mine, Donald Roberts, whom she had stolen from me when I went up north. We may have been toddlers, but bitterness seedlings need very little fertiliser to grow. And Cecilia was good with shit. She was dressed in jeans, a Ted Baker top, and a black felt hat pushed back on her head. Donald – a parody of Trendy Boy – was similarly dressed, with ripped jeans, trendy top, and Rae Bann glasses.

She greeted me as though there had never been a strangeness between us. Phoney, of course, to use Holden's favourite word in *The Catcher in the Rye*. She held me in a tight embrace for longer than she ever had in her life. Cecilia said she admired the art nouveau styling of my home. I explained it was art déco, a different period in art and style altogether, but she ignored me. She was good at that. The lounge, with cream-coloured walls, features fan shapes, and black lines stressing the period effect. There are two art déco red club chairs, one either side of a coffee table. It was a set Fred Astaire might have danced in. I'll miss my flat if I have to move.

[**Note**: *At this point in the statement, Catherine adopted a different voice for herself and Cecilia. For her sister's voice she used what might be described as an immature, girlish tone, often punc-tuated with giggles.*]

"More money than you know what to do with, sis?" Cecilia said. I was by now feeling more like Holden Caulfield by the second. I remembered how much I loathed the word 'sis', and so did she. Although there was some truth in her joke – I have expensive taste which I indulge – it grated on me. I introduced Elena to the two of them before returning to the kitchen. Cecilia joined me, almost tripping on my heels in her hurry. I knew she was after something; I knew she wanted to hurt me. She always has. First, she asked about Elena.

"She's lovely, your friend. What is she, Spanish, Italian?" What she meant was Elena was a foreigner. Lovely, my arse.

I told her she was of Greek descent but that she was born in Walthamstow.

"She's pretty. A special friend, is she? Nice legs. Just like

Dolores and Mummy?" That's what she said, her voice like nail-scraping-on-wall. She put her arm round me and hugged again. Twice in one evening. I would have smacked her then, but I knew she hadn't told me why she was here. She trawled her way through my spice rack, picking up bottles as I explained. Elena and I met when I was a consultant for *Médecins Sans Frontières* in Malawi. She persuaded me to take a post in Edinburgh when my tour ended. I said that she, like me, worked in the REH. And no, we are not lovers. My sister had been in the flat for ten minutes. Nine and a half too many. Then she got to it. Why she was here. She said in a voice that was all squeaky, girly and phoney. Phoney words, phoney voice, phoney bitch.

"Listen, there's news about Mother and Father. Mumser has finally got shot of the old man. She's moving to Dunbar, Scotland's Golf Coast, with the buxom Dolores as caddy. I'm afraid father is broke and may be heading your way. You were always his favourite, as you know. Child prodigy made good. He knows you're wealthy and is hoping you'll find room in this mansion for him. We knew that you were the golden child, so it's surprising that our mother left me the house. She knows you're loaded and the happiest of geniuses."

That shocked me. As the eldest, I should have inherited the house. She wasn't finished, though.

"Yep, lock, stock, and barrels of antiques. 'Twas ever thus, dear clever sister. They were both so desperate to hide their favouritism for you that I got all the goodies."

I know I was flushed then; I could feel my face burning. That was my house, where I grew up. With my stuff in it. I asked what she would do with it. If I got the chance, I'd have bought the place from her. It still had my stuff, and my childhood memories, and my childhood. What little there was of it.

"Going to get rid of all the junk and set up a commune. When I started a clear out, I found all our old stuff: your racing bike that you couldn't go was there. Old annuals, Cinderella Dolls, old pink duvet. And do you know what else? My *Lazytown* bike, the pink one with the glittery seat and bright ribbons."

She shouldn't have mentioned the bike. I can't remember what happened after that. I know stuff went on, noisy… Elena was there. Then Donald Roberts… and my car. That's all I remember. It's all I'm telling because I don't know what went on, apart from the noise. Then I was in hospital.

She shouldn't have mentioned the bike.

[*This concluded the third hypnosis session. Ms. Korda pointed out that her client appeared distressed and tired. She also advised that she would not consent to any further sessions.*]

Appendix 2

Statement by Inspector Deryck Jardine, Police Scotland, Edinburgh.

AT APPROXIMATELY NINE-THIRTY pm on 10th May this year, my officers were called to an apparent Road Traffic Accident at Rokeby Drive, Morningside, Edinburgh. What they found convinced them that this was a crime scene. One IC1 male – later identified as Donald Roberts, from Glasgow – was pronounced dead at the scene. The body had suffered catastrophic damage to head, torso, and legs. Members of the Fire Service were in attendance removing the body from the front of a silver Mercedes-Benz Class 3.0, registration NV16EKF. The driver was in a comatose condition in the driver's seat. An IC1 Female was removed from the car and taken to Edinburgh Royal Hospital. There was considerable damage to the garage wall of 17 Rokeby Drive.

Five witnesses stated they saw the Mercedes pursuing the IC1Male, driving onto the pavement, then crushing him against the garage wall. They further stated that the car reversed and further crushed the victim six or seven times. The witnesses' statements agree that the crash appears to have been deliberate.

Officers identified the driver from her car registration as Catherine Montague, a consultant at Edinburgh Royal Hospital. When officers attended her address – Flat 5A, 7 Marmion Crescent – they called in another crime scene. At this address, two further bodies were discovered. An IC2 female – later identified as Elena Stavros, a consultant at Edinburgh Royal Hospital – and an IC1 female, the driver's sister Cecilia Montague. Both were apparent victims of knife wounds. The first appears to have died from a single stab wound to the chest. The second, Cecilia Montague, suffered multiple stab wounds.

I have forwarded to the Procurator Fiscal my conclusions as follows.

I believe that the two incidents are related. At approximately nine o'clock, the first victim was stabbed in a violent, frenzied attack. The second victim, Elena Stavros, may have attempted to intervene, with resultant accidental death.

The third victim, Roberts, probably fled the scene, was followed by the attacker in her car, then repeatedly attacked, using the Mercedes car as a weapon.

I will therefore recommend that the suspect, Catherine Montague, be charged with two counts of murder and one count of manslaughter.

IT'S ALL ABOUT THE PATS

I used to have a goldfish called Barny. Although I don't remember his arrival, it must have been as a present for my birthday or Christmas, otherwise he would not have been swimming on the sideboard in my bedroom. Or perhaps my parents didn't like his smell. I was supposed to clean his bowl every week, but that seldom happened. His water got changed when I could no longer see him through the thick green sludge.

Barny must have had super-piscine genes to survive my custodianship. At various times his 'Goldflakes' were supplemented with a miniature Beatle – Ringo, I think it was – Campbell's tomato and lentil soup, fluff from between my toes, and chicken fried rice. Still, he got bigger and bigger. You won't notice fish getting bigger if you have them for years because they don't have growth spurts; they just occupy more and more space in the bowl. My mother suggested flushing him down the basin – 'to be with other big fishies' – but I knew all he would join would be wee, toilet paper and bulk family poo. Finally, when he could barely turn round in his bowl without scraping his fins on the side during a three-point turn, I insisted on buying him a rectangular tank. This was not much larger and was made of 'pressed steel and four-ply polystyrene', the label said. I looked it up: tin and plastic.

Anyway, silly Barny didn't adjust to life after the bowl; he just kept swimming round in the same direction as before, circling the tank. One benefit of the new container was that it took longer for the water to turn into green slime. By the time he went to the Great Aquarium in the Sky, he must have been nine or ten and six inches long. He had stopped being cute years before and latterly looked like a deflated whoopee cushion with raisins for eyes.

I remember crying when he did finally make the big drop and flush; I had found him that day upside down, having lost all colour. After that I pleaded with the family for another pet: can we get a dog/cat/hamster/budgie/warthog/pony/velociraptor depending on which Disney film I saw. The answers became more and more decisive and sharp. My mum sat me down and lectured me on the health risks and death-inducing quality of each: asthma, flu, lurgy, Black Death, spots. At my age, the last of these was the most sinister. The message got through. By the time I left school, I was so brainwashed that I refused to see my friend Ellen because of Joey. Loaby Dosser, the boxer, made Mary's house unvisitable.

I had now developed a phobic distrust of – almost paranoia about – animals. Yet when I went to the College of Textiles and Design in Peebles, I used orange, fish-shaped designs with black dots in many of my creations. In my second year, I produced an award-winning scarf, which was singled out for praise by a scout from Hermès in Paris. 'Why wait another two years to graduate, venez à Paris maintenant and we will enrich you immediatement.' Berenice Dubois was persuasive, sexy and a liar. When I arrived à Paris, they used my Barny design, charged €500 for a mini scarf and paid me a few centimes.

It took me five years to make it to the top of the design department, by which time I *was* enriched. I had risen to the upper reaches of the company, though not important enough to fire Bernice Dubois, the lying Parisian. By this time, I had an apartment in Avenue Montaigne on the 8th Arrondissement. My live-in assistant/ innamorato Jean found himself on the pavement when he brought home Chou Chou, his repulsive Poodle Française, with her glittery bow tie and unpleasantly brown bottom.

Like many obsessed with their own creativity, I now lived in a cocoon, avoiding the company of humans and animals alike. Charles Dickens might have written me into *A Christmas Carol* had I lived then. My god would have been textile design, rather than money. My disdain encompassed family, Jean the Chou Chou owner, and the textile machinists who turned my designs into scarves for the company. Like many Parisian artists and iconoclasts, I turned my apartment into a shrine to my creativity. I adorned my walls with framed thirty-centimetre square scraps of silk: Clair de Lune, Quadridge Perle, Voitures Exquises, and, of course, Barny.

Chosen by the company to tour the grand exhibitions around the world, I travelled to New York, Milan, London, and Atlanta. My travelling companion, the buyer, Claude, was selected because he was the least obnoxious I could find. The two months spent globetrotting throughout the exhibitions season were excruciating for me and possibly for him, though that was of no concern. Our last stop was Prague, a city about which I knew nothing. The Alchymist Grand Hotel, all that I wished to see of Prague, was luxurious and suited to the exhibition. The décor, however, with its attempt to create an art nouveau fantasy, was execrable, while the cuisine was best suited to the Big Mac 'n' Fries taste of our transatlantic buyers. As always, I spent the evening before the exhibition examining our display in minute detail. I also discussed with the models the deportment which I had decided best suited our products and the atmosphere of the Hall.

As I made my inspection, I stopped in front of a rather plain model, moved on, then came back to her. Assuming she spoke English, I stood before her, inspected her again and said, in a whisper, 'Why have you done this to my scarf?' With an especially stupid expression on her horsey face, she stammered. Perhaps she did not understand.

'Have you spat out some raisins? Have you broken a biro pen and wiped it with a €1000 Carre Taquin scarf? Idiot!' As the six-foot offender sputtered protestations of innocence, Claude arrived at my shoulder and sought to calm the villain who had defiled my design.

'Madame,' he breathed, 'what has the girl…'

'I am surrounded by imbeciles,' I said. 'Look! Look what she has done to my design. Send her to her kitchen where she belongs, serving soup.'

Claude removed the scarf and peered and peered again.

'Madame, perhaps we might retire to your suite to discuss the matter,' he said, taking my arm.

'Had I wished to be pawed by a minion, I would have asked that weeping person there. At least she smells better than you.' I said.

When we reached my room, I sat with a resounding whump on the faux Louis Quinze sofa. After Claude brought me a glass of the house champagne, he offered me his designer's loupe.

'Where is the flaw, madame?' he asked. Opening the company design folder, he turned to the relevant page and laid it beside the scarf. 'Madame, it is parfait. As you designed it.'

'Quelle peste!' I cried. 'Why did I allow you to accompany me?'

By now, even the compliant Claude's patience was exhausted.

'Madame,' he said, sighing before turning towards the door. He paused and turned back. 'I was the only employee in the Hermès Organization who was prepared to endure your company. Bon soir.'

I poured the foot wash champagne into the sink, before replacing it with a shot of St. Remy XO. Breathing mindfully to regain my composure, I opened my own loupe and examined the offending scarf. It was still there: the series of black dots on the upper edge which ruined my project. In a rage, I threw my glass across the room. For a moment, I tried to find sense in the situation. Was I surrounded by idiots, with no understanding of the intricacies of design, of the importance of minute detail?

I looked again at the pattern book. The same row of dots. Trying without success to replace my brandy glass on the side table, I turned the page to my Clair de Lune. La même chose. The same. The centime dropped.

'IT IS CALLED DIABETIC RETINOPATHY, and although in your case it is irreversible, we can slow the process. The total loss of vision can be delayed, perhaps for as much as two years,' Mister Harriman, Harley Street oculist pronounced. 'That will, of course, depend on some immediate lifestyle changes. The diabetes must be treated immediately. That goes without saying. You must stop work now to minimise the damage. Give up alcohol, smoking, reading; initiate a change of diet. This will give you time to adjust to a life... A life in darkness. There are organisations you must contact...'

I stopped listening.

HOPING that a return to my roots would somehow undo the oncoming blindness, I bought a house in Hyndland, Glasgow. In some illogical way, I felt that walking round the streets of my youth, visiting the exteriors of my primary and high schools, would clear my eyes of the encroaching grit-speckled clouds of grey. For months I pretended that the eye specialist was wrong, though I addressed the diabetic diet. Surely, I told myself, once I had that under control, the dots would cease to increase in size and might even clear. I would continue to work, though not with the Hermès Organisation. I might return to the Borders, perhaps setting up my own company in Selkirk or Peebles. Once the financial settlement had been agreed, I heard nothing more from my Parisian employers.

I heard nothing from anyone. No e-mails, no phone messages, no letters. Still refusing to face reality, I holidayed in Greece. A change of place would herald a change of outlook, would precede an improvement in ocular health. But the monuments were grey, the guides were unfocussed, the guide-books unreadable. When I returned to Glasgow's West End, I found only fliers for local tradespeople and election pamphlets behind the door. I assumed that's what they were, from the little I could read.

For a week or longer, I stayed in bed, getting up only for calls of nature and refills of brandy. I knew that the alcohol would kill me, exacerbating the diabetes and hopefully inducing a coma. It didn't matter. Since the age of seventeen, my world had revolved around art, creative design, intricate and innovative patterns. The realisation that my standing in the world depended on my genius, which I could no longer exercise, meant that there was no reason to get out of bed, no reason to exist.

I had in my mind a line from Shakespeare which made sense: *Then I defy you stars!* The stars which filled my vision, I would meditate away. I spent day after day after day attempting a meditative state wherein I would dissolve the black, menacing, developing stars which were destroying my eyes. I thought then of my funeral. Only one thought: no-one would come. My parents were dead, my former French colleagues were glad to say au revoir, the last friends I had were twenty years abandoned.

I did not know how the community nurse got my address; possibly the doctor treating my diabetes had alerted the service that I might be in need. When I admitted her, from what I could see, she was large and dressed in some pastel overall. Her face was featureless. I was sorry I had let her in; no-one was allowed into my world, ever. Not since Greece, not since Paris, not since any place or time I could recall. She tutted repeatedly, muttering about cleanliness and personal hygiene. She would return the next day, she said, to perform some cleaning function. I assumed she meant my house, but when, on arrival, she began to comb and cleanse my hair of 'the little pests', I evicted her with small ceremony. I assume she reported my case, because sometime later – I have no idea how long – another person arrived. Two. Medical, it sounded like. One psychiatric, the other clinical.

They gave me several injections and then a talking to. The problem with speaking to a suicidally inclined woman is that there is nothing you can say. Everything from 'putting this into perspective' to 'cheer up' is equally offensive. Yet I allowed myself to be bullied into accepting arrangements for twice weekly cleaning help. There was a condition though: I would have to submit to an intrusion of the 'let me plan to interfere in your life because you are now a blind person' kind. For a period of weeks, workmen interrupted my solitude to install bath rails, telephonic vibrating devices, and other blind woman gadgets. I refused, however, to have anyone help me leave the house. I would leave in a box.

The moment the different woman walking into the house, I knew something was wrong. Perhaps it was the smell, though I doubt that. I heard something. I couldn't place what it was, but I knew it was different. Something was crossing the floor.

Suddenly, I had the impression of two warm, soft worms resting on the back of my hand.

I screamed. Over and over.

'His name is…'

'Get it out!' I cried. 'I don't care what it's called, get it out! I hate them.'

'You frightened him,' the voice said. Before I could scream about being condescended to, she went on. 'He put his muzzle on the back of your hand. To show you…'

I lost all adult inhibitions, repeating at the top of my voice words I had last heard and used in the playground. Moments later, the door closed. A blind woman, owning a guide dog: death was preferable to such indignity. I cried all night.

Yet the following day they were back: the voice and the mutt. An animal which would cause asthma and flu and lurgy and the Black Death, and spots. This time it stayed further away, gently resting its body against my armchair. While I leaned away as far as I could, the voice explained the many ways in which 'he' would help me.

'I don't want to go to the shops or the library or church. I'll leave in a box, and I don't need an alien creature to do that.'

And still they persisted, the voice and the mutt. Again and again, it leaned against my chair, making no attempt to repeat the first day's intrusion. On the seventh day, I asked the voice, 'What is it? What kind?'

'He's a golden retriever,' came the answer. 'He is a year old, his coat is a beautiful blonde colour, and his eyes… his eyes would melt your heart.'

Just as she said that I felt a heavy warmth on my knee as he put his head there. Although I did not move him, I asked the obvious question. 'Why is he doing that?'

The woman sighed, a sigh which said: 'you are a sad and desolate woman.'

'He is showing that he would like to love you. Can't you feel that?'

I put my hand on his head. The first of ten thousand pats.

I did not leave in a box. We went to the shops; we went to the park; we went into the world. As Mister Dickens put it: Recalled to Life.

Barny and me.

ACKNOWLEDGMENTS

I would like to acknowledge the following for their help during the writing 0f this collection.

My family, for their patience and occasional silence
  Isobel Watt, Barbara Watt for proof-reading
  Lucy, for lying quietly at my feet. Sometimes.
  Members of Greenock Writers' Cub
  Members of Scottish Association of Writers

ABOUT THE AUTHOR

Anthony Watt was born in Glasgow, moving to Greenock to pursue a career in teaching. Thought his career, he produced many musical shows, as well as writing and producing pantomimes.

His historical novels are set during the lifetime of the Roman Republic, then Empire, and during the American Civil War.

Much of his writing features strong female characters, while his short stories often have a macabre tone and feature surprise endings.

Facebook: Anthony Watt Author

The Imperial Coin Maker During the barbaric reign of the Emperor Caracalla, the hero, Zeno, is recruited by the empress to produce propaganda in the form of coinage. Zeno, however, has a troubling destiny which is only revealed to him by the Germanic Princess Adela

Winner of the 2020 Scottish Association of Writers Award for historical fiction.

Available at: amazon.co.uk/dp/B08B32KJLB

Caesar's Gladiatrix tells the story of Iryna, the mysterious eastern gladiatrix, recruited by Julius Caesar. Having saved his life from pirates, she is sent for training to the richest man in the world, Crassus. When she becomes invincible in the arena, she is then given the task of organising Caesar's gladiatorial games. The bloody conclusion brings Rome to the brink of civil war, and sees Iryna proscribed for death.

Available at: amazon.co.uk/dp/B09DJ9V29

Seven men to make a Shadow. A collection of sixteen short stories, a number of them award-winning. Characters include Jack the Ripper, Walt Disney and sundry ghosts and witches.

Available at: amazon.co.uk/dp/B08628K7LM